LIAR, CHEATER, SINNER, SAINT

LIAR, CHEATER, SINNER, SAINT

MEGAN CARNEY

PREVIOUS TITLES BY MEGAN CARNEY

Sarina, Sweetheart

Navy Trent Series
Trap and Trace
From Hackerville with Love
Humans, Practicing
Domestic Threats

Learn more about Megan Carney at megancarney.com.

Print ISBN: 979-8-9999781-0-3
E-book ISBN: 979-8-9999781-1-0

*This book is dedicated to anyone who's
made a mistake they can't take back.*

PROLOGUE

Kevin
Washington, DC, 2023

"I KNOW WHY I'm here." Kevin knew he had to speak first. Let them know they hadn't surprised him. He had friends too.

"I haven't even introduced myself," the man said.

Who this man was wasn't important. Who had sent this man was the real question. But answering the second question required getting through this interview mostly unscathed. Kevin *did* have friends. Well, Kevin had people who owed him favors.

"Denton Carlisle," the man said. "From OIG."

Office of the Inspector General. Kevin had sent cases to the OIG before. He had managed to avoid being a case until now.

Denton placed one hand over the other on the conference room table. A thick gold wedding band glinted just below a swollen knuckle. Hereditary high blood pressure, someone had told Kevin. He had to learn meditation just to keep from giving himself a heart attack.

Whatever the cause, Denton's calm was unnerving. Kevin doubted he could provoke Denton into making a mistake. There was no point in introducing himself. Kevin's name and everything the agency knew about him were in the files open on Denton's laptop.

"You have some questions about the Hong Kong operation," Kevin said.

Denton started the recording. "If you're ready to begin."

"I am."

CHAPTER 1

Dan
Hong Kong, 2015

HONG KONG IS where businessmen go to cheat on their taxes and wives. It suits me fine. Any of my ex-wives will gladly testify that monogamy isn't my strong suit. As for governments and their precious taxes, I think more people should cheat. My record as an average tax-paying citizen didn't help when the US kicked me out five years ago.

I heard a little too much under a dingy roof in Philadelphia. A little too much about a man with more connections and money than I could ever dream of having. So much for democracy. Being kicked out of my birth country felt like a divorce, actually. Lady Liberty offered me a large, one-time alimony payment in return for never stepping in the Western Hemisphere again.

My whiskey glass is empty. I don't remember finishing it. I don't remember whether it's my fifth or seventh drink of the night. In exactly three minutes a man called Tiny

Clint will walk through the door of this posh, velvet-and-mahogany bar. Tiny Clint is neither Tiny nor named Clint. His bosses call him "Tiny" because they watch too many gangster movies. He added Clint because he prefers spaghetti westerns. He fancies himself an intellectual Chinese cowboy. He's more intelligent than most enforcers I know. It doesn't bode well for me.

In approximately five minutes, April will come—might come, if she isn't fed up with me. I order another whiskey. The bartender eyes me like I've already overstayed my welcome.

Yeah, I'm a cliché. An alcoholic, Irish ex-cop with a self-destructive bent and a paunch, who ended up on the wrong side of the law. There's a reason for most clichés. Being a cop is the worthiest, shittiest job I know. I spent a lot of time around bad people trying to protect good people. There's only two ways to survive a job like mine: create convincing delusions of your own sainthood, or admit you're not a saint at all.

I'm no saint.

I take a sip of my whiskey just as Tiny ducks his enormous form into the bar. He's somewhere between six and seven feet, especially rare for a Chinese man. When he's not out eliminating Hu's business rivals or guarding drug shipments, he's on the weight bench in his apartment. Tiny could rip a telephone book in half, or me, without breaking a sweat.

When Tiny's eyes find me, the bartender holds out his hand so I can settle my tab. Everyone knows Tiny Clint around here.

The stool next to me creaks as Tiny settles in. "Dan."

"Tiny." April will come, even though she said she wouldn't. I recognized the tone in her voice on the other end of the line; it's the same tone of voice I use when I say I won't have another drink.

"You know what my orders are?"

"Take me out for a nice night on the town? I hear there's a revival of *Cats* showing tonight."

Tiny shakes his head. "I like you, Dan Mackenzie. You could make this easier on yourself."

It's true that we've developed a sort of friendship. Tiny is pragmatic and efficient when it comes to his work, and I admire that.

"It's a good offer," Tiny says. "A lucrative offer."

"Assuming I make it."

"There is that."

I spin the whiskey glass in my shaking hand. Amber shadows reflect off the polished bar surface. A dark knot in the wood blinks at me balefully. "I hate to damage our business relationship, but I can't do this job. I know how I survive; I'm a cockroach."

Tiny looks confused. "Is that some sort of Kafka reference?"

"I survive because no one cares enough to squash me." Now is not the time to mention all the times I've played snitch. "If I take this job, I'll need protection from someone. I'll have to choose a side." For all its modern weaponry, organized crime runs on a feudal system. Independent operators can only be so successful. Bigger jobs require swearing loyalty to a king to earn a space inside the castle walls.

"If you were Hu's man, I could protect you."

"If I were Hu's man, I'd be a criminal."

Again, Tiny looks confused. "Aren't you already?"

Perhaps he's right. Maybe I crossed the line years ago, snitch or not.

"Think of it as career development."

A harsh laugh catches in my throat. "That's what the chief told Brian."

"Who the hell is Brian?"

"This guy I went through Academy with. Smart guy, when he thought with his head. Took up with the chief's wife after he started on the force." I push my glass away. April hasn't come. Liquor won't help now. Still, my mouth keeps moving to delay the inevitable. "One day we're called into this convenience store robbery-turned-hostage situation, and the chief orders Brian to take point. The chief used those exact words, 'career development.' Right before Brian was shot for getting in over his head."

Out of the corner of my eye I see April enter. She sees me and Tiny, and nearly leaves again. Tiny drops a large arm over my shoulders. "Last chance. Do you want the job or do we take a ride?"

April is three steps away, two. Tiny isn't paying attention to the slim college student with red hair and flashing green eyes.

A whiff of April's perfume tickles my nose as she bends Tiny's arm behind his back, forcing his wrist forward and twisting the hand. It's called the chicken wing; we used it on the force all the time. You can subdue a suspect without causing permanent damage. Before Tiny can recover from the pain, she delivers a solid kick to the base of his spine. His chin connects with the bar as he falls between the stools and the polished mahogany, trapped.

April presses a knee against Tiny's spine, holding his head so he's staring at the gleaming dark wood. His nose is crushed against it. Looks painful.

"When I find out who you are—" Tiny is cut off by his own cry as April leans more of her weight against him.

With one hand, she pulls out her phone. The case for her phone is a stun gun. Her professor helped her apply for the weapons permit so she could carry it when she travels around to do research for her thesis on the economics of urbanization. Just last month, she spent two weeks in the New Territories by herself, interviewing former residents of Kuk Po.

"I'm no one in this town so you won't ever find me," she says. "Dan Mackenzie is no one too, as far you're concerned. He works for my boss now, not yours. Got it?"

The few other people in the bar studiously keep their eyes on their drinks. I think Tiny nods; it's hard to tell.

"Leave Dan alone. And don't come looking for me. Think of me as Medusa. You don't want to see my face."

April's trash talk is a little highbrow sometimes. It's a good thing Tiny actually knows what she means. She presses her phone case against Tiny's back and activates the Taser. Tiny jerks but doesn't lose consciousness. April frowns and tries again. This time his eyes roll back into his head. She lets go. His body, still breathing, falls against the metal circles at the base of the stools. His nose is a little off-center, a small trickle of blood escaping from one nostril.

"Tha—" I start to say.

"Shut up."

I probably deserve that. April isn't a likely bodyguard. She could hold her own in an MMA ring, but she keeps most of her fights in the dojo. She's also my niece. She's only in Hong Kong for a semester doing her study abroad program. I reach for my whiskey and she covers the glass with her hand. "Fallen off the wagon again, I see."

"Never really hopped on."

She sighs. "We're leaving."

"Where to?" I like this bar. It's disappointing I won't be able to come back for a while.

"Somewhere they don't serve liquor."

CHAPTER 2

Dan
Philadelphia, 1989

I IRONED MY uniform the night before my first day of work as a cop. I made sure the creases were perfectly aligned on both pant legs. I laid my shiny new badge and black leather gear belt on the dresser. I woke up with plenty of time to spare and arrived on my first morning fifteen minutes early.

I presented myself, scrubbed and shaved and polished, to the lieutenant in his cramped office. My careful preparations only earned me a grunt. "Your partner isn't here yet," he said. "I'll find you when he gets here."

The squad room was crowded with desks of assorted vintages and beat cops lounging with cups of coffee. I was too shy to insert myself into one of the social circles, so I took a seat in the waiting room. The only seat left was next to a woman filling out a police report. Tears leaked quietly down her cheeks. A purple bruise circled her wrist. Gray hair streaked through her dark, short perm.

I couldn't help it; I glanced over at the form. When I saw the word "rape" I looked away. She looked up and noticed my uniform.

"Could you help me?" she managed. "I'm trying to remember. Is it a burglary or a robbery if they break into your house while you're home?"

I shifted in my seat, unsure what to do with her distress. "Robbery."

Her hand shook as she transcribed my answer, making the word nearly unreadable. Most of the handwriting on the form was illegible. Her report would go nowhere. The desk clerk was too busy to help her. I didn't have the stones to get someone from the back room.

"Let me get you a new form," I said. "If you just tell me what happened, I'll write things down for you."

It was an effort to keep my own handwriting steady as she recited her story. Her name was Elsie. Three days ago, her home had been broken into, and she had been raped. It took her four days to work up the courage to leave the house to report it. Her attacker had worn a mask and gloves. He only spoke in a whisper. It was dark. He stole her TV, VCR, and most of her record collection. The only identifying detail she could give was that his breath smelled like garlic.

As we were finishing the interview, the lieutenant approached with a man even I would describe as tall, dark, and handsome. The lieutenant looked between the red-eyed woman and me. I couldn't tell if he was pleased or upset.

"Everyone else seemed busy," I mumbled. I felt my

starched collar bite into my neck as my head drooped. "I was just writing things down for her, really."

Elsie looked down at her lap. I realized, belatedly, I'd made her feel ashamed again.

"Glad he could help you, ma'am," the lieutenant said. "I'll take the report, if you don't mind, and in a few minutes an officer will be out to see you."

My new partner and the lieutenant led me to a pair of desks in the squad room. "Dan Mackenzie, meet your new partner, Mack Danson."

Someone snickered behind us. The similarities between our names became a popular running gag. "Mack and Mack Daddy" was generally the favorite. Sometimes it was "Mack and Mack" or "M & M," which was a short jump to "S & M," after the shift had ended and drinks were flowing.

When I first met Mack, I idolized him. I thought "Mack Daddy" referred to his dashing good looks and smooth charm.

The lieutenant looked over the report, then frowned. "Might as well give this to Lewis. A female officer will make her feel better, but there's nothing we can do."

"What do you mean there's nothing we can do?" I asked.

"It's his first case," Mack said. "Might as well let him follow through with it."

The lieutenant shrugged. "All right. It's yours."

I repeated my question while Mack skimmed the report.

He brushed a lock of dark hair, slick with hair gel, back into his carefully styled swoop. The squad room had gone quiet around us. "How would you proceed with this, junior Officer Mackenzie?"

I was in a fishbowl. Half of the squad room, some smirking, some sympathetic, had turned to observe my first teachable moment on the force.

"Canvas the neighborhood." My voice sounded loud to me, but my observers leaned in to hear.

"The attack was late at night and he came in the back door," Mack said. "Odds are nobody saw anything."

"But what about the physical details?"

Mack cleared his throat, then put a hand on my shoulder. "All she could give you was a guess at the eye color and estimated height. Witnesses are notoriously bad at physical descriptions. Basically we're looking for a white man between five and six feet, with eyes that are blue or green. You see the problem?"

I couldn't believe that her pain wouldn't be answered by justice. That gathering the courage to leave her house and make a statement meant nothing.

"Did you smell her?"

I jerked my head up, ready to call my new partner a few choice names.

"I didn't mean it that way," Mack said. "I just meant, I could smell her shampoo when I walked up to her. She showered away all the trace evidence. Since she waited four days to file her report, we can't collect DNA."

My anger, though misdirected, was slow to fade. "You said we would follow through."

Mack studied me, then clapped me on the back. "I think I like you, Dan Mackenzie."

We wasted a morning canvassing the neighborhood. Mack was right. No one had seen anything. At my insistence, we even visited a few of the local pawnshops. Her VCR and TV were too common to trace. Elsie's report ended up in the dusty pile of unsolved cases. I was the only one who benefited. The lieutenant noted my initiative, and a few years later I was put on the detective track. I almost made it.

CHAPTER 3

Dan
Hong Kong, 2015

IT'S HARD TO be alone in Hong Kong; it's impossible in Mong Kok. It's like New Year's Eve in Times Square all the time. Even at one in the morning, every building is dressed in neon signs advertising what's for sale. Food. Clothing. Handbags. Knockoff handbags. Electronics. Knockoff electronics. Other things are for sale in the small, dark alleys surrounding the main streets; things you don't want to write home about.

I follow April past a wire rack hung with taut inflated plastic bags. Each one is half full of water. It's a goldfish stand. Here, goldfish come in multiple colors. Owning one is supposed to bring you good luck. I tried it once. My goldfish only lived a week.

April ducks into an alley off the main street before I can stop her. She's been here long enough to know better. Most of the brightly lit areas in Mong Kok are safe enough; it's the dark corners where shadows jump out at you.

"April!" I call.

She turns, motions me on, but doesn't stop. I hurry to keep up. As I pass the corner, I feel a fine, wet spray on my face and hands. I don't need to step under a streetlight to see what it is. I can smell it. Fish blood. I look to my left and find the source. A fishmonger standing over a headless glass-eyed fish. In his hand, a large knife sticky from use reflects the neon lights.

"Sorry, sorry, mister," he says, nodding.

It's a nice act for the tourists. I swear at him in Cantonese.

He drops his smile and adds a few words to my vocabulary, waving the knife over the bloody cutting board.

Someone yanks my arm. It's April. I didn't even notice her coming back. She pulls me away, past more shops and bright lights. My whisky-fogged brain registers the streets vaguely. We take a circuitous route through the shopping hotspots, ending near the Ladies Market. A stall brimming with a rainbow of silk, satin, and taffeta wedding dresses. She looks around, satisfied, then lets us drop to slower pace.

At a quarter to two, she gives up trying to find a place that doesn't serve liquor. She settles for a hotel restaurant and the table farthest from the bar. It's the kind of place that tries to be a one-stop shop for every specialty in Hong Kong and does none of them well. As the waitress comes up, I'm wiping fish blood from my face with the fancy cloth napkin.

Her nose wrinkles. She's looking at me like I just walked

in with dog shit on the bottom of my shoe. "Perhaps I could get you another napkin, sir."

April orders dim sum for two, even though I say I don't want anything.

A plate of fat pork and chive dumplings arrives. My mouth waters, but I don't want her to know she was right. She drops a dumpling on a plate and pushes it across the table. I push it back. I might be drunk, but I'm not a child.

"Fine," she mutters. Two dumplings later she speaks again. "I can't do this for you anymore. This time I mean it." She stabs her chopsticks into the scraps of gray meat. "My semester ended a week ago. I fly home in a few hours. Or did you forget?"

"I didn't forget." I wait for her to put the pieces together, glad dumplings don't require knives.

"This isn't some low-level gangster like the rest, is it?"

I'd call myself all sorts of names right now if I had the energy. I can't help worrying about tomorrow, when I'll find out if April was enough to scare Tiny off. I don't have any other tricks up my sleeve. The bottles of liquor behind the bar gleam at me seductively.

She kicks my shin so hard my eyes tear. If this is what it feels like when April holds back, I might owe Tiny an apology.

"Look, I'm sorry." I lean down to rub my shin. "I didn't have anyone else to call. You'll be on a plane in six hours. They can't touch you then."

"What the hell did you get me mixed up in? I'm telling Dad when I get home."

"Only if you want to play bodyguard again."

She glares at me.

"Like you said, it's the last time," I say. "You're going back. I'm stuck here. End of story."

"You could move. The settlement money would buy you a cheap shack on a beach in Bangkok."

The lawyers for Mr. High and Mighty drew up the paperwork to make it look like the money I accepted was a lump sum from the department not to sue for wrongful termination. I shake my head. I used the last of my savings to set myself up in Hong Kong. I haven't touched a dime of the settlement money. I won't. It's blood money. "Nothing I do here is illegal. Technically."

"People with legal businesses don't have as much contact with gangsters as you do."

I do anti-private investigations. It's a little niche I invented that doesn't keep me up too much at night. Tax evasion is a national pastime in Hong Kong. It's cheap to register a corporation here. People with money pay to have byzantine corporate paperwork drawn up that hides their assets. I get paid to test how well their trail is hidden.

Basically, I charge hourly to run through the kind of investigation a federal agent might do, but instead of giving the results to the authorities, I let my clients know how well protected they are. It's not honorable work, but it pays the bills. Aside from a couple of little fights April has settled for me, it's relatively boring.

"You owe me an explanation," she says.

The waitress comes over and asks if we want something to drink. April cuts me off with a look. "Just refills on our waters, please."

I pick at the dumpling on my plate. It's not bad. Since she won't let me order a drink, I might as well put something in my stomach.

"Well?" she asks.

"I thought you didn't want to be involved."

"I'm not involved. I'm leaving in the morning."

My stomach mulls uncertainly over the few bites I've taken. "One of my clients wants me to do a job. I don't want to. Let's leave it at that."

"Not good enough," she snaps.

I gulp water just to feel something cool on my throat. I'm nearly sober now. I don't like the feeling. "They want me to fake some background checks. Make it look like a reputable company did them."

"And this is where you draw the line." Her sarcasm cuts deep.

"Yeah, it is." The tables around us are full of business people, couples up late. People living happy, normal lives. People who can have one beer and stop. I'm thirsty for a six-pack. "This isn't work I normally do. They're offering to pay me a lot of money to do a job outside of my expertise. It means they want someone expendable. Someone who won't be around to collect."

She traces swirled patterns in the condensation of her glass. "So leave. Go to that beach in Bangkok. Or Taiwan. Or South Korea. Anywhere else."

"It's not that simple."

"Nothing ever is with you."

The jazz tune in the background changes to something

with more piano, a staccato rhythm that upsets my threading pulse. This is why I prefer not to be sober.

"Do you know how they plan to use the background checks?"

"It's not important." I think Tiny's boss wants to start a bank. The IRS is forcing any bank that wants to do business in the US to declare any assets belonging to US citizens, to cut down on tax fraud. Of course, a bank run by the Little Caesar gang wouldn't care about lying for their clients.

April tilts her head, considering. "Your clients know you as a guy who does financial investigations."

"I said it's not important. You're right. I shouldn't have called you."

"And you said background checks, not background check. So someone unscrupulous who works in the financial sector wants you to make a group of people look legitimate."

She's too smart for her own good. "Just drop it. Please."

"This must be related to those new IRS regulations you were telling me about. The ones that require foreign banks report the assets of US citizens."

I lick my dry lips. "The less you know the better."

"Your friends want to start a bank with crooked management for criminals to hide their money."

"Oh, I'm sure they'll want some legitimate customers too. Just to confuse the regulators."

"There's no solution to this equation. You have to leave."

"That whiskey is catching up to me." I head toward the bathroom, careful not to look back. Medusa isn't a bad comparison for her sometimes.

I do my business, wash my hands, then splash cold water on my cheeks. No, my jowls. I think I can admit that now. An overweight man in his fifties has to stop pretending at some point. The stubble of my beard is gray. My hair was red like April's once.

This is more depressing than our conversation. I leave the florescent lights of the bathroom for the dimness of the restaurant. There's a man leaning over April, younger than me by ten years and better dressed. His swagger and his suit say he wants people to know he makes a lot of money. The sway tells me he's drunk.

She sits stiffly, leaning away. He's not taking the hint. The douchebag touches her shoulder, lets his hand linger. She doesn't need me to defend her, but I can't stop myself.

"I have the penthouse," I hear him say as I get closer. "I'll order some champagne—"

She flicks her shoulder-length hair in her face. "I have a boyfriend."

He recovers quickly but continues letting his eyes rove. He's noticing all the things I never notice about her because, well, we're related.

"Bugger off," I say. There are a lot of British expats in Hong Kong. They've rubbed off on me.

"This is the boyfriend?" he asks, clearly unimpressed.

"More like chaperone," I say.

"Look, honey—"

This time I reach his hand before he can touch her. He forms a fist; I wrap my hand around it and squeeze until his face is pinched with pain. There's a feeling bones get just before they break; if you've been on the giving or receiving end of enough beatings you recognize it. It's like the bone tries to become a liquid before it realizes it can't. Then it just snaps.

"Uncle, that's enough," April says.

I release him with his hand intact; he cradles it against his chest. It'll be sore for the next few hours.

He looks at April, sneering to cover the tremble in his wrist. "You're not worth it anyway."

April rolls her eyes as he stumbles away. "So you can defend my honor but you won't lift a finger to save yourself?"

"Yeah. Something like that." I recognize pity in her expression. I'd rather have her angry at me. I pull a few bills from my wallet and drop them next to the soy sauce. "Have a good flight. Tell your dad hi for me."

CHAPTER 4

Dan
Philadelphia, 1989

I WATCHED HOW William manned the grill with pride. A new gas grill with a bright red cover. William had bought the grill to celebrate winning a big account for his construction business. He was always happy when business was going well.

Summers in Philadelphia are normally humid, but that day even the weather cooperated. William's life was going according to plan: he was a successful businessman with a picture-perfect family. He didn't know—I didn't know—that one uninvited guest would change everything. For both of us.

April was six, maybe. It's hard to remember exactly. She had ginger pigtails, a gap-toothed smile, and freckles on her nose.

"Spin me again!" she demanded.

I held her wrists tight, careful to be well clear of the

sizzling burgers and swung April in circles. She was still giggling when I set her down, unsteady on her feet.

"Again!"

"I think maybe you need a break. You seem a little dizzy."

She shook her head, swaying a little.

"I think he's right, sweetie," said Marge.

April stuck out her tongue at her mother, then ran off toward the jump rope discarded next to the back door.

I sat down next to Carol and took another gulp of my beer. She hid her frown, then moved the beer farther away. Marge took note, but she didn't say anything. At the time, it annoyed me. Sure, I drank a little more than the average person. I also saw a little more than the average person. I decided to let it go.

"Food's ready!" called William.

"Hot dog or burger?" I asked Carol.

She smiled. "One of each."

I loved her appetites. She ate with gusto. She gobbled up books and hobbies. She found something to laugh about every day. I, on the other hand, often needed 2 beers to get to sleep. Hours spent marinating in your thoughts will do that.

I heard Mack arrive before I saw him. He had what could kindly be described as a gaggle of children. I had a hard time keeping their names straight. The gaggle turned the corner first. The children naturally gravitated toward April and her collection of Hula-Hoops and jump ropes. Then I saw Mack with his wife. And someone else who looked vaguely familiar.

Not from the force. Maybe from the news?

"Dan, Carol, I'd like you to meet Mayor Holden," Mack said.

It explained why he looked familiar. I shook the mayor's hand by rote. His grip was cold, even on a summer's day, but strong. Mack had mentioned he knew the mayor, but I had chalked it up to bragging. Over six months of being Mack's partner, I had discovered his liberal definition of truth.

"I hope you don't mind one extra," Mack said. "He has a little business proposition for your brother."

"William won't mind." If it was good for business, William would be happy. William's business was everything to him. At the time, he was building houses, but he was hoping to move into commercial projects. It wasn't so much about the money for him, I think. It was about achieving success, respect. "I'll introduce you in a few minutes."

Once the food had been distributed and the grill was cooling, I brought the mayor over to William.

"Mack brought a friend," I said. "This is—"

William smiled broadly. "Mayor Holden, of course. We don't normally have guests of your caliber in our backyard."

The mayor waved the praise away with studied humility. "I'm here today asking for your help."

"Well, any favors I can do for the city, of course." No doubt William was thinking of how such favors would translate into influence when bidding for government contracts. I didn't begrudge him that. Still, it struck me as odd at the time that a big man like the mayor would seek out a small player like William. My new cynicism hadn't gone unnoticed by Carol.

The politician's smile didn't inspire my confidence.

"I've had some good luck in the stock market," Mayor Holden said. "I'm looking for a good investment."

Mack leaned behind the mayor's back and gave me a thumbs up, like I should be happy about this. Something smelled wrong. If only I'd taken the time to dig a little deeper then. But I'd only been a cop for a year. I didn't know how to investigate financial crimes. I didn't know how to find out where the mayor's money had really come from.

"Mack says your brother talks about your business all the time," Mayor Holden continued. "About what a good businessman you are. That you're looking to expand."

That last part was true. I had mentioned his plans; I had never bragged about William's business skills. It wasn't that I thought William was bad at what he did. It just felt patronizing.

William raised his eyebrows as he looked over his shoulder at me. "You want to invest in Mackenzie Construction?"

"You have a good reputation," the Mayor said. "I wouldn't want to work with someone who didn't."

Later, I understood why William's reputation as an honest businessman was so important to the mayor. All William heard was the compliment.

"Would you like to see my plans?" William asked. "I've been eyeing a few rundown commercial properties. They're eyesores but the land's valuable. They would make great retail locations if they were redeveloped."

"While we're eating?" Marge asked. "Finish lunch first. Mayor, can I get you something?"

The mayor ate two hot dogs and a hamburger. Despite Marge's protest, the conversation never strayed far from business.

I pulled William aside. "Be careful with this one. I don't trust him." I didn't explain that I had never talked up William's business skills. Seemed best not to start that argument.

William, predictably, didn't take it well. "You're still treating me like I'm your little brother. I don't need your protection."

I gave up too easily. William spent the next hour inside with the mayor, laying out his expansion plans. What William didn't know, what I couldn't have known, was that the mayor's money was not from trading stocks. He was taking substantial bribes from the mob. Ten years later, the mayor had become a governor, then a senator. William's business had grown so much he was concentrating on management, not accounting. And the new accountant for Mackenzie Construction was a personal friend of the senator. Mackenzie Construction was laundering the Honorable Senator Holden's ill-gotten money.

CHAPTER 5

Dan
Hong Kong, 2015

A RINGING PHONE stabs at my eardrums. I roll away from it, then press my face into the pillow. No one will have good news for me today. My own breath forces me out of bed; even I can smell the vodka. Whiskey is my medication of choice, but the stash at my apartment was down to dregs. It feels like it must be early. I'm so tired my head aches. I try to focus on the red numerals of my alarm clock. No, it's afternoon. I let the call go to voicemail and stumble to the bathroom.

My reflection isn't pretty. A puffy face with red eyes and gray stubble on my chin. A couple drops of fish blood decorate my left earlobe.

The phone rings again. I shut the door and brush my teeth.

On the third call, I check to see who's so damn eager to talk to me. My brother William, April's father. We haven't talked in years. Most—make that all—of our conversations end in arguments.

William doesn't wait for me to greet him.

"What the hell did you do this time?" he yells.

I look at the empty bottle next to the bed. A half-pint of orange vodka, apparently. "Good to hear from you too, Will." My little brother used to go by Will until he got his MBA. Then he switched to the more regal, more douche-bag-like William.

"Don't play cute with me." He'd reach through the phone and strangle me if he could.

"Why don't you tell me what I've done to piss you off this time so I can congratulate myself?"

"You're unbelievable. Un-fucking-believable." He pounds his fist on something in the background. "I knew when she said she was going to study in Hong Kong you would screw it up somehow."

"This is about April?" A tremor creeps into my voice.

"What happened exactly?" my brother sneers. "You went on another bender, and April felt like she had to make sure you didn't swallow your vomit in your sleep?"

If only.

My brother fills the silence. "April didn't make her flight. I talked to her while she was packing yesterday. Everything was fine. She was going to meet you for a drink and then go to the airport. The airline says she never even checked in."

Cold sweat gathers in my armpits. Sure, I knew there was some risk. More than usual. But the job was about tax dodging, right? Worth waiting a day and then killing me. But worth the effort of tracking down April in the few hours before her flight? My tumbling thoughts won't slow down. They took April. They might have killed—no, they wouldn't. Not without finding out who she worked for. Tiny's smart. A quick glance at the last name on her passport would make clear that she's family. The threat against my life didn't buy my cooperation, so he's going to threaten something more valuable.

"Say something," my brother spits into the phone. "Did you hear me?"

"Yeah, yeah, I heard you. We—uh—met for a drink, like she said. She left around two a.m. to pick up her stuff." There's no point in going into the rest. The last thing I need is my brother catching a flight here to take on the criminal underworld. "Something must have come up at the last minute with her thesis."

"She would have called."

"Just calm down. I'll go by her apartment and make sure she's okay."

"I. Will. Not. Calm. Down." My brother likes to use extra words to make sure you know he's smarter than you. "Marge and I are flying out." Then with deep sarcasm, "Do you think you could manage to meet us at the airport?"

"Hang on, you don't need to do that." Getting April back alive will be hard enough. Trying to protect William and Marge at the same time will only complicate things. "I'm sure it was a last-minute change in plans."

I hear William take a slow hissing breath. "My daughter has a 4.0 GPA. My daughter has earned black belts in three different martial arts. My daughter would not miss her flight when she has an interview for her dream job tomorrow."

April didn't mention it. Course, I didn't really ask either. I pinch my arm, hard, to bring myself back. "I'll call you in a couple hours. Don't buy any tickets yet."

"You have one hour."

Subtlety is not my brother's strong point. If he starts "investigating," he'll get April killed. "Fine. One hour."

I hang up and call Tiny.

"I thought I might hear from you today."

I can hear a smirk in Tiny's voice.

When I was just a cop, before I was an alcoholic, before the first divorce, my brother once asked me how I could handle the pressure. *People live or die based on your decisions. How do you keep your head on straight?* I told him I just do. It's the truth. There's something wonderfully clarifying about a life-or-death situation. The chattering, nagging thoughts in my head are quiet. My training tells me what to do, and I do it. "Put her on the phone."

"There are a few things we need to discuss first."

"Put her on the goddamn phone, and then we can talk."

"You're awfully demanding for a man in your position," Tiny says.

"Your kidnapping skills are rusty. Negotiations don't start until I have proof of life."

A lone ant has found the dried sugar patches at the lip of the orange vodka bottle. I watch him scurry back to tell his friends as the silence stretches.

A sudden background noise hisses over the line. Tiny put me on speakerphone.

"This is all your fault," April says.

There's no defense against her words. She deserves an abject apology; it's on the tip of my tongue. But I can't appear weak in front of our audience. "I know." I squeeze my eyes shut, then lean against the wall. "I'll do the job for them, and they'll let you go." The images I drink to keep away form a slideshow on my eyelids. A little black wire being taped to my chest. A little tic in my partner's face when he figures out I set him up. My bruises, his bruises, bones breaking, and then an exploding circle of red. I snap my eyes open.

"It'll take a while," I say. "But I will get you out of there."

"I know." She says the words simply and firmly, without any doubt or disbelief. I wonder what I have done to earn her trust.

"Satisfied?" Tiny asks.

"For now."

"You seem to understand the terms. No calling the police; we have sources, we'll know. When the work is completed, she gets to leave."

"Unharmed," I growl. "She gets to leave unharmed."

"I will stay with her."

As if that's supposed to make me feel better. But there's something odd in his tone. Like he's serious about wanting to protect for reasons beyond business.

"I need two weeks," I say.

"Take your time." He's smirking again—I just know it.

"I want a daily photo with April holding *The Straits Times*."

"We'll drop it off in your mailbox."

Lots of criminals are going back to old-school methods to avoid leaving electronic evidence. "One more thing, she has to call her dad and say she needs extra time to work on her thesis."

"That's out of the question."

"She missed her flight home. They're worried about her. If she doesn't call, he'll fly out here and raise a stink all the way to the chief secretary." Hong Kong used to have a governor. When the Chinese took over, they changed the title and the job duties. If it sounds like a demotion, it is.

"You can call him," Tiny says.

I hate to air my dirty laundry in front of him, but there's no way around it. "He and I aren't that close. He has to hear it from her. Within the hour."

"You want me to lie to Dad?" April asks incredulously. She sighs. "I don't know if I can."

"I'm sorry, April." *I'm sorry about everything.* "You have to."

"You're a real piece of work," Tiny says. This coming from the bastard who just kidnapped my niece.

I hang up. I'm April's only chance. She deserves better. I replay the short conversation in my head, looking for any clues. There are none. I'll have to concentrate on more immediate problems. I need to get April's belongings from her apartment, before her roommates start asking questions.

I collect the objects necessary to pass for ordinary from the various piles sitting around my room: a shirt that doesn't smell too much, pants that aren't too wrinkled, shoes hiding under the bed, and socks with holes safely hidden at the heel.

A splash of water against my face, a few swipes of deodorant, and I head toward the door. On the other side, I hear the familiar jangle of my roommate's keys. Tom's a decent kid.

My finances require a little help with the rent. Middle class in Hong Kong means two people in a five-hundred-square-foot apartment. I share a three-hundred-square-foot apartment with whomever I can find to sleep on the couch. College students, undergrad in particular, make the best roommates. They're too self-absorbed to spend much time thinking about my schedule. Also, they still think binge drinking is a recreational activity so I don't get any lectures.

"Oh sorry, man." Tom squeezes past me.

"Don't worry about it. I'm on my way out."

"You all right?"

This is the longest conversation Tom and I have had since I rented him the place. "Um, yeah. Why?"

"Your eyes look red. If you have allergies, I have some powdered—"

"No, thanks. I just took something." Tom is big into weird remedies. He's always mixing the ground-up horn of something or the dried, powdered sex organs of something else into his morning coffee. I try not to open his side of the cupboards. It smells funny.

My cell phone rings as I close the door behind me. The sound doesn't stab quite as much as it did half an hour ago. Until I look at the caller ID.

"Morning, Whitney," I say with forced cheerfulness.

"It's afternoon."

This is one person I can't afford to be rude to. "Afternoon, then. What can I do for you?"

"I was hoping you could meet me for a late lunch. Or an early breakfast. Depending on where you are in your drinking. Hot pot, my treat."

It's only her treat because someone else is picking up the tab. "Today is kind of busy. Could we meet next week?"

"I cleared my schedule just for you. I'm hurt you won't do the same." She doesn't sound hurt at all. If anything, she sounds like a cat about to pounce on its prey. The kind of cat that doesn't ever kill the mouse, just bats it around.

It'll take me an hour to get to April's apartment and back. I can't meet Whitney while hauling around April's stuff; it would lead to awkward questions. "I could meet you in two hours," I say, knowing Whitney will force me to rush.

"You'll meet me in ninety minutes. At the Lucky Dragon."

CHAPTER 6

Kevin
Washington, DC, 2023

KEVIN GATHERED INGREDIENTS from his almost empty cupboards: fried peanuts, dried shrimp roe, dried squid. Then from the refrigerator: deep-fried fish maw, fresh ginger root, green onions, roasted duck, cilantro, a covered metal saucepan still half-full. Finally, he set out the things he'd bought on the way home from his second "interview" with Denton Carlisle: grass carp, fried youtiao.

Congee was a great comfort food. He'd been living on it all week. He set the saucepan on the stove. A knock on the door startled him as he reached to turn on the burner. He wasn't expecting anyone.

Least of all, Navy Trent. He watched her through the peephole for a moment, trying to read why she was here. She stood up to her full five-foot-six height, but not rigid. Not relaxed, but not worried. They weren't friends exactly.

Or enemies. He'd been her handler on one operation, but she wasn't a field agent.

She couldn't possibly make this day any worse. He opened the door.

"Took you long enough," Navy said. She took her shoes off and walked toward the smell of dinner.

He hadn't invited her to sit at his kitchen table. "Please, make yourself comfortable."

"I came early," Navy said.

Kevin didn't have plans with anyone tonight.

"I wanted to warn you," Navy continued.

"Warn me about what?" Kevin looked at his carefully arranged ingredients. He'd planned to spend the next forty-five minutes assembling the perfect bowl of Sampan Congee.

"Saul is coming too," Navy said.

Fuck. Kevin didn't need to deal with two assholes this week. "What the hell does Saul want from you and me?" But even as he finished the question, he knew. "When will Saul be here?"

"Half an hour," Navy said.

Kevin could make a slightly less than perfect bowl of Sampan Congee in thirty minutes. "Then you're helping with dinner."

Navy smiled slightly. "Okay."

"Turn that burner on medium heat and keep stirring. If the porridge starts thickening up, add a little water."

"This is congee." Navy's hand paused, stuck on a memory. "You made me this on that operation in Romania."

"Good comfort food." Same thing he'd told her then. "You have to keep stirring or it'll burn to the bottom."

Navy moved the spatula in slow deliberate circles. "You made this for me when I was upset."

"Like I said, good comfort food."

"Fine." Navy sighed. "Don't tell me what's going on."

Kevin set the grass carp on a cutting board. *Cut in quarter-inch slices, then lay flat.* Kevin had watched the chef at the congee place in Hong Kong a thousand times. He'd watched so intently that on one quiet night the chef had let him come behind the counter to learn. Too intently, Kevin understood now. He had made himself memorable. Not the only mistake he'd made on that operation.

Now that the fish is laid flat, cut horizontally just below the surface. Almost like buttering a piece of bread. Kevin lifted the first slice of fish, so thin it was almost translucent, and set it in the bottom of the bowl. The pieces were so thin, pouring the hot congee on top would cook them. There was enough for two.

"Have you eaten?" Kevin asked.

Navy shook her head. "Saul grabbed me on my way out the door."

Kevin took out a second bowl. A sharp knife, just under the top layer of flesh, was the key to this technique. Soon, neat piles of perfectly sliced fish nestled in the two bowls. Five minutes spent. He washed the cutting board and started on the ginger.

"Kevin, I—" Navy started.

Kevin peeled the earth-brown skin to reveal the pungent, sharp yellow root inside. This must be cut like matchsticks. But very small, because otherwise the flavor would be too strong. And don't add too much.

"Goddamnit, Kevin." Navy looked up from the porridge, but didn't stop stirring. "Will you please tell me something?"

The green onion split down the center as he sliced it. Spring onions would have been better, and more traditional for the dish, but the Asian grocer he went to didn't always have them. He minced the stalk, perhaps more forcefully than necessary.

"I helped a bad man a long time ago." Kevin sprinkled ingredients into bowls: small handfuls of the dried squid he'd been soaking, flakes of roasted duck, bright green crescents of onion.

"And?" Navy asked.

"And then I didn't help him. And for a while, that wasn't a problem."

Navy's mouth tightened in frustration. "And then what?"

"And then power shifted."

"His friends are upset with you," Navy said. "How powerful are they?"

"Powerful enough." Kevin set two bowls next to the bubbling porridge. "You can fill these now."

Kevin took the filled bowls from Navy and added the final touches, a sprinkling of dried shrimp roe, fried peanuts, and cilantro. And, of course, thick slices of the fried youtiao breadstick.

"We should eat before Saul gets here," Kevin said.

Navy took a hesitant bite then her eyes widened. "This is . . . really good."

Kevin smiled. "Worth the wait."

"Saul will help you," Navy said. "That's good, right?"

"He'll help me to help himself," Kevin said. "As long as he thinks he can keep the deal we made secret. If he thinks I'm discredited, he'll claim I acted on my own." Kevin savored a spoonful of his creation. The smooth texture, the perfectly cooked fish, a slight tang from the ginger, umami from the squid, and the crunch of the peanuts.

"Saul must know I'm not going to tell," Navy said.

"Saul wants more than your silence. He'll want your help."

Navy frowned. "With what?"

"I don't know," Kevin said. "But you shouldn't get your hands dirty."

"I know we're not exactly friends. But—"

"My decisions, my consequences." Kevin leaned forward; he let his anger show. He wanted to intimidate her. *My karma,* he finished the thought in his head. He had gone back to Hong Kong as Jones to fix his mistakes. He had made so many moral compromises when there were no good choices; he wasn't sure what he deserved.

CHAPTER 7

Dan
Hong Kong, 2015

WHITNEY SPOTS ME at the door, taps her watch, and shakes her head. She's not alone. Two bad signs. She never had a partner in any of our previous meetings. The tables are set far apart, each cocooned in its own circle of light from the lamps in the ceiling. Far enough away a hushed conversation wouldn't carry. It was the type of restaurant set up for doing business. After the bright afternoon, it takes my eyes a second to adjust to the dimness.

Her briefcase is tucked neatly under her chair, a fancy leather model that boasts a designer label. Either IRS field agents are paid better than I thought, or Whitney frequents one of the knockoff stalls at the night markets.

The male next to her wears a surly expression and a suit commensurate to a government salary. He's a white man somewhere in his thirties. His dress, his manner, and his haircut are all generic.

I drop my sweaty self into the third chair at the table. I've never adjusted to the oppressively humid heat, and I've just hauled three heavy duffel bags from April's apartment to mine. I wait for Whitney to introduce her friend; she doesn't. Fine. There's a plate set out for me, with a glass of water next to it. I drink half the glass in one chug.

"This is your source?" the man asks. He has sharp, pale blue eyes that seem to memorize my every movement. His Cantonese is flawless.

Whitney smiles and sips her hot tea, leaving red lipstick on the rim of her cup. "Looks can be deceiving." In Whitney's case, they definitely are. She's a forty-year-old woman who uses makeup and blond in a bottle to look thirty. It works from a distance.

She and I have an arrangement. I throw her a bone every once in a while—the name of an American client hiding cash—and in return my brother is left alone. She's why I can't leave the country. While Internal Affairs was investigating my partner, they discovered that Mackenzie Construction was laundering money for the corrupt governor. The IRS was duly informed. I'm not sure how much William knows; I doubt he would have agreed to the arrangement. I do know that tax-dodging charges would destroy his business and bankrupt his family.

The man stares at me, waiting for me to speak. I finish my glass of water. I've been trained in interrogation too. He'll have to show his cards first.

"We've been hearing some rumors from the criminal underground," Whitney says.

It's so cute when she tries to use criminal lingo. The

only time she gets away from her desk is when she asks me for another name. Normally, though, she doesn't use the royal "we."

"I'm Dan Mackenzie." I reach across the empty plates, scattered with crumbs, and offer my hand to Whitney's new partner. They started on appetizers without me.

"Call me Jones." He doesn't accept the handshake.

"Uh-huh." Now I'm sure of it. Jones is a federal agent, but not IRS. The IRS is fairly new to the game of overseas field offices and agents. This man has a deliberately neutral demeanor, cultivated to make him as forgettable as white bread. Whitney's new "partner" is CIA.

"Our new laws have been very effective in reducing the number of undeclared foreign bank accounts," Whitney says. A few years ago, the IRS succeeded in passing a bill regulating foreign banks. Any assets held in the United States would be frozen, unless the bank agreed to share the records of US citizens. Tax-dodging billionaires everywhere scrambled. Most large foreign banks have caved in order to keep doing business in the US.

"Congratulations," I say.

Annoyance flickers across Jones's face. "There are rumors that someone wants to start a bank here to act as a front for illicit transactions. A bank that would lie for its clients."

Hopefully, this is all they know. I frown, like I'm thinking the idea over. "That'd be hard to do. The regulatory agencies require background checks on all top executives."

The smile on Jones's face chills me. "Background checks can be faked. Rumor is they're going to hire an expert."

An expert? I'm flattered. I stay silent, waiting for him to show his hand.

"Someone with experience investigating financial crimes."

So he knows my background. Not a surprise, I guess. "Neat idea. This is the first I've heard of it." If Tiny gets word someone is sniffing around, he'll go into cleanup mode.

"Let me be more specific." Jones leans forward and speaks more softly. If anything, lowering the volume sharpens his tone. "There's a rumor the Little Caesar gang wants to start a bank using background checks faked by you."

Shit. I'll just have to tell him the same thing I told Tiny. "That kind of work is a little out of my league."

Jones taps his fingers against the lacquered red table. "But if you hear anything, you'd call, right?"

"Of course."

It's a good thing my face is already coated in sweat from the afternoon's exertions. Jones dissects my expression, looking down his beak-like nose. There's a hint of a smile on his thin lips. His features are pinched in the center of his face. His close-set eyes and nose make him look like a bird of prey.

"Is that all?" I ask. "I'm not really hungry."

Whitney frowns with pursed red lips. "I know our previous deals have been rather casual."

If you consider threatening my brother's family with financial destitution casual.

"But it really is important that you cooperate with us. This is about more than dodging taxes. It's about terr—"

Jones cuts her off with a nasty look; she withers in her seat. "What my partner is trying to say is that this case is important to our superiors. We're getting a lot of pressure to find a lead."

Interrogation 101. Alternate threats with pretensions of friendship. If Whitney had been about to say terrorism, it would explain why Tiny suddenly got into the kidnapping business. I put on my best Boy Scout face. "I suppose a bank like that could be used by all sorts of criminals."

Jones glares at Whitney, then me. "Yes."

The waiter arrives with three plates and a large steaming pot of water. The pot goes on the burner, already warm, in the center of the table. Herbs and spices spin and twirl as the water heats to bubbling. The plates hold the raw food to be cooked. Whitney has a plate of chicken and vegetable chunks. Jones has a pile of shaved red meat. For me, they ordered the mysterious undersea special. There are white chunks of what appears to be chopped octopus tentacle. I can see the suckers. Two whole, tiny octopuses—no bigger than a child's fist—stare at me as they garnish the plate. They're so fresh I swear I see one tentacle moving.

What really makes my stomach turn over is the pile of shrimp. These are not the neatly peeled and deveined shrimp found in shrimp cocktails. These are whole, still in their shell, with their beady little eyes and scratchy, thin legs.

I hate seafood, and Whitney knows it. Jones is enjoying this. I remind myself it's just an interrogation tactic. Make the room uncomfortable. Demonstrate your control by forcing the suspect do something he doesn't want to do.

Fuck him. They obviously think I'm more useful to them running around, otherwise I would have been picked up extraordinary rendition style. "Well, I'd love to help. But I don't know anything. I'll call the minute I do."

"Enough games," Jones says.

I'm halfway out of my chair when Jones pulls me off-balance. He holds my arm near the red-hot burner, close enough to cause pain, far enough away not to leave a mark. Definitely CIA. The thing with twerps like Jones is they think their skills make them so much better than the rest of the world. They're always surprised when a less worthy opponent fights back. I might be out of shape, but I weigh more than him. And he's off-balance now too.

I dig my fingers into his wrist and flip our arms so the back of his hand touches the burner. He swears, releases me, and jumps back. The scent of singed hair tickles my nose.

Jones is still cursing my mother when the waiter appears with a cold towel. "Please, sir, sit. It doesn't look bad. I will lay this over it. You must be careful." The waiter scurries away from Jones's glare.

I'm about to leave when Jones speaks.

"There's something you should know." The threat in his tone is no longer veiled. "This isn't just official business." He removes the washcloth, folds it carefully into a square, and sets it on the table. The burn on his hand has bubbled into a curved line of small blisters. The pain doesn't seem to bother him. "Taking down Hu and the Little Caesar gang is a personal mission for me. I'll see it done with or without your help."

Whitney looks at me, almost apologetically.

Jones continues without missing a beat. "You help me, and I'll see to it you make a soft landing. You don't help me, and you'll get whatever you deserve."

It's clear what Jones thinks I deserve. If it weren't for April, I'd let him have his way. I should say something clever to show he hasn't rattled me, but he has. They don't know April was kidnapped, or they would offer a quid pro quo. Jones has limited resources for his operation; that's the only explanation for why he hasn't wiretapped my phone. A lack of support won't stop a man with Jones's determination, though. Sooner or later, he'll resort to desperate measures. I have to get April out before then. I leave without saying goodbye.

CHAPTER 8

Dan
Philadelphia, 1991

THE CALL THAT ended my first marriage came on the night shift. A woman called to report a loud party in her neighborhood. She knew the parents were away for the weekend. She told us the street and driveway were crowded with cars. We didn't rush to the scene. It was just some misbehaving teenagers, after all. The neighborhood could kindly be described as rough. Twenty minutes later, we finished our steak and egg specials at the late-night diner.

The roads delayed us too. It was a cold winter that year. So cold that night, salt on the roads didn't help. We slipped and slid our way there, counting the spinouts and accidents along the way. Duty bound us to slow down at each one and make sure there were no people in danger. One person had already died from exposure that weekend.

We flipped on our lights when we reached the block of

the offending house. Predictably, teenagers streamed out the door and toward the cars lined up on the street. We let them pass. Mack sat down the teenager who lived there for a stern lecture while I looked around for anyone who needed help. I found a girl in leggings passed out on the couch, her puffed bangs smashed against the cushions. I found another boy emptying his stomach in the upstairs master bathroom, the knees of his whitewashed jeans stained by his own vomit.

We hustled both of them into the back of the squad car after calling their parents. This time we were in a hurry. They stank up the car. The boy smelled of vomit and the girl looked ready to spew any second. We were starting the car, about to head to the station, when the nosy neighbor tapped on our car window.

Mack rolled his eyes at me before letting the window down. "Good evening, ma'am. Things should be a bit quieter now."

I could tell her housecoat and her hairstyle, disheveled as it was, came from a different era. To be honest, I felt a little sorry for her. We saw it all the time in these run-down neighborhoods. Older people, usually widows, who had bought their houses when the neighborhood was working-class instead of dangerous. Unwilling or unable to move, they spent their retired days peering out their windows trying to keep the neighborhood from degrading any further.

"You see that house?" She pointed a wool mitten at a decrepit-looking house next door to the party house. Even in the dark, I could see the foreclosure notice tacked to the door. A dirty for-sale sign hung crookedly in the front yard. The house had been on the market a while.

"Yes, ma'am."

"I saw smoke coming from the chimney earlier. I think someone moved in. But I know it hasn't sold."

"Yes, ma'am," Mack repeated. "We'll check it out."

"Thank you, officers." She tightened her housecoat with mittened hands. "Now I can finally get some sleep."

Protocol dictated that one of us should stay in the car that stank of vomit, probably me, considering I was the junior officer. I looked back at our charges, sobering up in the back. "We have your driver's licenses. If you're not in the car when we get back, you'll be charged with fleeing a police officer in addition to underage drinking."

They nodded, though the boy had a squirrelly expression.

Mack added a little more persuasion. "If either of your cars is missing when we get back, we can add drunk driving to the list."

Mack opened the door; cold air rushed in. The girl shivered.

"Most people who die of cold exposure are drunk," Mack said. "The alcohol makes you feel warmer than you are."

I think Mack made up that first part, but it did the trick. We left the squad car running to keep them warm, and half-heartedly moved on to our next assignment.

"Junkie in an abandoned house," Mack said. "Our first bingo hit this month."

Every month a new bingo sheet circulated around the station: prostitute on the corner next to Tom's Tobacco and

Gas, drug dealer on a playground at midnight, car stolen outside 13 Lucky Ladies. We'd arrest someone then a couple months later I'd pick them up doing the same damn thing. For the first few years I mocked the repeat offenders along with everyone else. Later, when my badge had lost its shine, I wondered if we were part of the problem.

We found the back door of the foreclosed house jimmied open. The smell of a wood fire hung in the air. A cold wind pressed at the creaky joints of the house. It was only marginally warmer than outside. Our flashlights illuminated the evidence of neglect, one bright yellow circle at a time. Rodent feces in the corners. Vandalism in the hallways. The only sounds of movement we heard were small feet that skittered inside the walls. We followed the smell of woodsmoke to a living room. There were, as the neighbor suspected, people there. Red coals that had long since failed to give off warmth glowed in a fireplace. Two strung-out addicts, a man and a woman, were passed out on a thin mattress on the floor.

When I pressed my fingers to their necks, it was clear they weren't just passed out. They were dead, faces frozen in bizarre smiles.

"Jesus," Mack whispered from across the room. I was surprised; dead addicts didn't normally shock veterans on the force.

I followed the beam of Mack's flashlight to the object holding his attention. A crib, hidden in the shadows of the room. Walking over to Mack, I was simultaneously repelled and pulled closer. In the center of the crib a small child, no more than six months old, lay still as a stone. She wore a clean, pink knit cap. Her Cupid's bow lips were blue. Crystallized tracks sparkled on her cherublike cheeks. Beneath her small head, I saw a dark spot on the threadbare paisley-flowered sheet. I felt it with two fingers. The cold, stiff fabric melted in circles under my touch. The baby's tears. Frozen. The coroner calculated her time of death was close to the time we got the call from the nosy neighbor.

What got me in the end was the contradictions in it all. We did some perfunctory investigation of the addict parents to find next of kin. Even the hardened, cynical counselor at the clinic told us they were working hard to come clean. They were trying to be good parents. Physical examination of the scene bore that out. The baby's diaper had been changed recently. Her clothes were clean. The parents bought one hit from the wrong dealer. The drugs were contaminated. They died, the fire ran out, the music was loud, and no one heard the baby cry. That was Mack's summary in his report.

He neglected to mention that we could have arrived at the scene sooner. I didn't dare correct it, being the junior officer.

The night I signed the report, I finally broke down. My shift ended late, so Carol was asleep when I came home. I stared at her prone form for several minutes, wondering if I should wake her. As pathetic as it sounds, I just wanted someone to hold. Finally, I went down to the basement, where I had my workshop. Lack of activity kept it clean. The only piece of equipment I used regularly was the mini-fridge where I kept my beer. I turned on the TV, hoping to find some late-night movie to distract me from my guilt. I didn't have any illusions. Time of death reports are always approximate. Maybe we could have saved the child, maybe we couldn't. But that wasn't really the point, was it?

I started crying before I even opened the beer. I heard footsteps upstairs, listened to my wife carefully walk down the hallway, open the basement door, and pad down the stairs. Her steps paused at the closed door to my workshop. I was still crying. I don't know if she was aware I had heard her or not. She never came in.

Many years later, after our divorce, I remembered that moment as the night our marriage ended. I didn't ask for support. She didn't offer any. Everything else that passed between us was window dressing.

CHAPTER 9

Dan
Hong Kong, 2015

THANKFULLY, TOM IS gone when I get home from the meeting with Whitney and her "partner." It's time to work on April's ransom. The couch is covered with Tom's things. My room isn't much neater. I end up at the small kitchen table, staring at the blank, mocking pages of a notebook. My closed laptop waits expectantly. The problem is, I didn't pay much attention when Tiny made his original proposal. After the first sentence, I knew my answer would be no.

I think back to the night Tiny outlined the job. At the same posh bar where April beat him up. They were playing some modern orchestral music with discordant violins. We had a table instead of our usual spots at the bar, at Tiny's insistence.

Tiny called it a piece of cake. Easy. lucrative work, he promised. Instead of following the trail, I would just create it. I can hear his voice in my apartment. I don't like it.

I have to get the details right.

We just need you to make up a few background checks. I knew better than to ask why. When I didn't say anything at all, Tiny continued by holding up a hand with his fingers spread out. *Five background checks for executive-type positions. Four men, one woman.*

I complimented him on being progressive. He said having one woman was his idea because women were under-represented in upper management. I hid a smile. In Tiny's mind, breaking the glass ceiling on the criminal underworld probably did seem like an egalitarian cause. I thanked him for the opportunity and turned it down.

He looked confused, then upset. *You don't understand. Hu is not asking. Five background checks for executives. Four men, one woman. They should be educated in the West. England maybe, or the United States. A work history that is unremarkable, but shows experience in finance.*

I turned him down again. That pained expression came back to his face. *This request is directly from Hu. No one says no to Hu. I don't want to hurt you. I consider you a friend.*

Hu is Tiny's boss. Well, the boss of the whole Little Caesar gang. What Tiny said wasn't technically true. People have said no to Hu. It's just most of them didn't survive the experience. The Little Caesar gang grew by absorbing other small operations in hostile takeovers. Hu runs a motley, but efficient, collection of criminal enterprises ranging from money laundering to drug running, and even dabbles in weapons smuggling.

Enough distracting myself. I rewind the memory back to Tiny's questionable declaration of friendship.

I don't want to hurt you. I consider you a friend.

Then don't hurt me. Find someone else. This job is out of my league.

Tiny outlined the job again. Five background checks for executive types. Western-educated with experience in finance. There was something else beyond that, though. A specific skill set for each one. The remnants of my hangover hold the memory hostage. I close my eyes, grit my teeth, and try again.

I see Tiny's face, earnest, trying to convince me to cooperate. *The bank must look viable,* he said. *One person must have a background in investing, an MBA and a resume with management experience. The type of person who could be a CEO. Are you listening, Dan? You should be listening carefully.*

I was drinking an old-fashioned with bourbon. A maraschino cherry perched on the ice cubes. I could still taste the tang of bitters and orange on my tongue as he spoke. I think I mumbled some sort of refusal again.

Tiny pretended not to hear me. *Another person must have experience in marketing. There should be projects on their resume that demonstrate modest success. Remember, no one should stand out. It should be plausible no one has heard of them. A third person should have experience in accounting and auditing. The kind of person who might be a CFO.*

My memory fades like a projector with a dim bulb. I look down at my scrawled notes. It's not enough. Each executive had a specific set of skills. I only have details for three of them.

Pressure builds in my forehead as I try again.

An old-fashioned with bourbon. A cherry on top. A

gangster who thinks he will save my life by getting me to take the job. *So we have a CEO, a marketing guy, and a CFO. The fourth executive should have a law degree. The sort of person who could be a general counsel. The fifth executive should have a resume focused on operations, logistics. The sort of person who would be a COO. That stands for Chief Operations Officer.* Here Tiny puffed up with pride with his new vocabulary.

I replay the conversation from the beginning over and over, until it isn't just Tiny's voice in his apartment. I can almost see him, sitting at the table across from me with his large, surprisingly baby-like, hands. All my notes fit on one page. April's life rests on my scrawled handwriting and shaky recall. I replay the conversation again, but give up halfway through. My imagination is beginning to overtake my memory.

There's a funny thing I noticed about witnesses on the occasions any of my cases went to trial. On the first interview, most witnesses are tentative. It's hard to recall details, especially if something didn't seem important at the time. But on the second, third, and fourth telling the witnesses get more confident. They will swear, do swear under oath, to being absolutely sure of what they had seen. The retelling of the story becomes the story, changes the reality.

My cell phone chimes. It's my brother again; I let it vibrate for a few rings. Answering it feels like reaching for a live snake.

"Afternoon, William," I say.

"April called and told us not to worry." He doesn't sound angry. Yet.

"See? I told you everything was fine. I found her at her apartment and told her to call."

"She didn't sound like herself."

I stab at the notebook with my pen. It leaves a cluster of black dots on the page. I imagine they're bullet holes in Tiny's chest. "You want me to check on her again?"

He huffs into the phone. I imagine his nostrils flaring, like a bull about to charge.

"I want you to pick us up at the airport tomorrow," William says. "Our plane is about to take off."

Shit. "You're overreacting. You're going to spend twelve hours on a plane just to learn she's fine."

Our fragile peace shatters. "Are you her father now?" he snaps. "Marge and I are coming. I already texted you our flight information. You have a guest room, right? We'll stay with you."

Just like my brother to assume I want to host his royal highness. I'd warn him my guest room is a couch, but I won't be able to keep tabs on him if he stays anywhere else. "Sure, I can pick you up."

I hear a flight attendant telling William he has to turn off his phone. He hangs up without saying goodbye.

Tom, my roommate, will have to go somewhere until I get April released. A hotel, I guess. Though, one night at any hotel close to my apartment is a stretch for my budget. Unless I use the settlement money. The large, one-time alimony payment given to me when I agreed to renounce my United States citizenship.

I feel my dead partner's glare. The payment has always felt like blood money to me. Sure, I didn't know that I would end up killing Mack when I wore the wire to get the evidence against him. But it was my gun that shot him.

His nickname was "Mack Daddy" for a reason. He had a weakness for beautiful women, and handsome, devilish good looks; he was rarely turned down. As a married man, that led to problems. Specifically, blackmail problems with the local mobsters. They reeled him in, bit by bit, until he was tipping them off every time we were about to serve a warrant.

I tell Mack's ghost that I'm not using the money to help myself. It's for April. William's good intentions could easily get April killed. The specter haunting my psyche is unsatisfied.

Fuck Mack. He's the one who screwed up, not me. It's not like I wanted to set him up. I didn't have a choice. And now I need the settlement money to help April. I'm going to use it.

I force myself back to the notebook. Tom won't be back until late, and my brother won't be here until tomorrow afternoon. There's a ransom to finish.

"Yun-Fat Tsang," I write at the top of a blank page. I make a list of the things I looked at as an investigator when reviewing background checks: education, credit history, employment history, references interviewed. At first the details come slowly, then too fast for me to write down. The next time I look up, several hours have passed. My laptop is open; I have a professional-looking template to fill in with my notes. I even have the first draft of an interview with Yun-Fat Tsang's Yale college roommate.

I stretch, feeling lightheaded. Of course I'm lightheaded.

I didn't eat lunch and the time for dinner passed hours ago. White cardboard containers of takeout clutter the fridge. I choose one that isn't the oldest and isn't the newest. It's some sort of noodles, I think. As I bend down to retrieve it, a stabbing pain attacks my temples. The door creaks as I clutch it for balance. The woozy feeling doesn't pass. Withdrawal symptoms. I haven't had a drink for nearly a day. The craving for the sting of hard alcohol is real. I open every cabinet, swaying on my feet, sparkles dancing in my vision, desperate for the elixir that will make my symptoms go away.

God, I'm pathetic.

My niece is in the middle of a crisis, and I'm looking for my next drink. I microwave the leftover noodle something-or-other. The beep as the timer runs out feels like an icepick at my temples. I sit back down at the table to work. Yun-Fat Tsang graduated from Yale with a degree in—

I've never had a headache that hurts this much.

Yun-Fat Tsang graduated from Yale with a degree in economics. His first job out of college was—

Just one bottle of whiskey. A small bottle. The store isn't far away. Or I could buy it by the glass. The bar isn't too far away either. A little time away from the computer would do me good.

No. Yun-Fat Tsang's first job after college was—red clouds my vision until the next wave of pain recedes—a bank shift manager. Then, three years later—I grit my teeth, hear myself groan.

I can't operate like this. I'll quit alcohol, I promise myself. Just not today.

Tom has beer in the fridge. Normally, I wouldn't touch it. The alcohol content is too low, and he always buys the cheapest swill he can find. It'll have to do.

It looks like pee. I hate that it tastes good. I hate how the headache, the wooziness fades at the first sip. After one beer, my stomach will accept food. After two, I can work again. No wonder my brother despises me.

The rough draft of Yun-Fat Tsang's background check is finished by the time I stumble to the bedroom. But that's just the report. All the supporting documents will have to be faked as well: copies of school transcripts, a birth certificate, a marriage license. Other things, too, that I'm too tired to think of right now. Tom isn't home yet; I'll have to deal with him later.

The buildings outside my window glitter with lights. Behind one of those lights, on Hu's orders, Tiny holds April hostage. I know how this will end. I know how it has to end. I'm only preparing a ransom for April. Her freedom for my life. And really, that wouldn't bother me so much, except that Hu has an artistic soul when it comes to how he kills.

Last year, the police found Hu's accountant stuffed into a large, wide-mouthed vase with small diamonds pressed into his eyes and his hands bound. Apparently, the accountant was skimming a little off the top. The vase was decorated with scarlet and gold fish, a unique and intricate design that nobody could track to any manufacturer in the city. Fish are a symbol of wealth. Red is the color traditionally associated with good fortune. The art Hu created for the vase was both an insult and an homage to Chinese tradition. Red is rarely seen at funerals, because it is supposed to be a symbol of happiness. It's rumored that iron oxide was found in the glaze used on the vase, perhaps from the accountant's blood. Collectors are already lining up in anticipation of the police auction. The basic message was clear.

Covet Hu's wealth, and you will die a rich man. I'm not sure what sort of end will be arranged for me. I just hope April never hears the details.

CHAPTER 10

Dan
Hong Kong, 2015

THE CHEP LA Kok airport was designed with a theme I call industrial hospital. The predominant colors are white and steel. Mostly white. Lots and lots of white. The upper floors feel modern and airy thanks to dramatic, sweeping structures of glass. In the windowless baggage claim area where I'm waiting, I'm more reminded of the morgue at the Philadelphia PD. Or it could just be my nerves.

Last time I saw William was five years ago, and we didn't part on good terms. He thought I was running away after Mack's death. William idolized Mack. He still thinks Mack died in a gang shootout. I figured the official cover-up would be easier to swallow than the truth; that William's idol was a two-timing sleazebag who sold his soul to the mob and was about to kill me when I shot first. Mack was the big brother William had always wanted. I don't have the heart to tarnish William's memories with reality. The only reason Mack's marriage survived until his death was because his wife stuck her head in the sand.

The man walking toward me is practically a stranger. My brother has aged. Why not? I have. His thick, sandy red hair has thinned at the temples. A trim, middle-aged woman follows behind him. Marge has aged more gracefully. My brother scowls a lot. The lines on Marge's face show kindness and laughter. She'll make a good grandmother, if I can get April out of this alive.

William inspects me, pausing for a second at the flab hanging over my belt. I know I look like shit. For one thing, I didn't sleep more than three hours last night. And I haven't had my morning drink.

"I wasn't sure you'd come," he says.

"I keep my promises." I sound belligerent. All I wanted him to do was put a little faith in me.

"Yeah. Well." He's rescued by the first of the bags arriving on the carousel. "There's mine." His strides are purposeful, more aggressive than necessary to push through the crowd. That's my brother. Always focused on a goal.

Marge folds me into a warm hug. "Daniel."

She's called me "Daniel" since we met. I'm not sure why, even my birth certificate says "Dan," but I don't mind.

"It's good to see you, Marge." It is. Marge never approved of my drinking or my affairs, but her approach to problems is to kill them with kindness. My brother yells until the problem goes away. I went away. I guess you could say his approach worked.

William reappears with two roller bags. "This is all our luggage. Take us to April's apartment."

I was prepared for this. I rehearsed my story all the way to the airport.

"April called me while you were on the plane; she said a last-minute interview opportunity came up for her thesis. She found another resident of Kuk Po."

My brother looks blankly at me.

"The area was abandoned in the fifties when most of the families left to find jobs in cities." I'm surprised I can remember that much. Every time April starts to talk about her thesis, my brain stumbles over terms like 'Nash equilibrium,' 'joint supply,' and 'Gini coefficient.' "Anyway, she said she'd be back in a couple weeks."

"We can just call her," Marge assures her husband.

"Actually . . ." I delivered my fair share of bad news while I was on the force. I once told a mother that her husband and two children had died in a car accident on the way to a soccer tournament. I told a middle-aged son that his senile mother froze to death in a blizzard because she had wandered away from home. I told a husband that his wife had been raped, then stabbed to death and left in a dumpster. Telling my brother his daughter, my niece, is fine is harder than all of that.

"Actually what?" snaps my brother.

"She called me because her cell phone was nearly dead; she wasn't sure she'd be able to charge it where she was headed. She said she'd call as soon as she can."

My brother eyes me skeptically.

I paste on a smile. "Don't let the city fool you. There are still areas in rural Hong Kong where an electrical outlet is hard to find."

"If we don't hear from her by tonight, we're going after her."

I'll have to think of another diversion by then. My brother's lips are pressed thin; he's going to argue with me no matter what I say. Maybe I should put him on the train toward Kuk Po. It's the one place I know April isn't. I shrug, like it's no big deal, take the roller bags and turn my back to as I walk toward the train terminal.

For a blissful five minutes, my brother says nothing. Then he notices where we're heading to the metro station. "You don't have a car?" he asks incredulously.

"William, please," Marge says.

My brother has never lived anywhere but the suburbs of Philadelphia. It still amazes me that he lives twenty minutes from one of the most populous cities on the East Coast, and thinks homelessness is a problem that happens elsewhere, the drug war is over, and second amendment issues are solely about hunters and guns. He used his success to insulate his family from the evils of the world, then forgot they existed. I try to make a joke of it. "It's like New York. No one drives because the traffic is so bad." Jokes aside, it makes even less sense to have a car in Hong Kong than it does in New York. Forget the costs of driving it and maintaining it, a parking spot in the city is nearly as expensive as an apartment.

I cut in front of my brother before he tries to use the machine to buy metro tickets. The fare system is a bit confusing for newcomers. No, let's be honest, I want to show him I can be useful.

It doesn't take long enough to buy and print our tickets.

Once that's done, there's nothing to do but wait for the train in the thick silence. They only come every twelve minutes.

"You can have my bedroom, and I'll take the couch," I say. I left a note for my roommate with cash for the hotel. William shakes his head. "Of all the places to settle."

He's right, of course. For someone on the run, Hong Kong offers few advantages. The cost of living is expensive. In addition to local law enforcement, several other countries have field offices for their regulators here. Like, say, the IRS. Had I known landing in Hong Kong would lead to meeting Whitney, I would have opted for somewhere quieter. When I chose the flight, I wasn't planning to stay. Hong Kong was just the gateway to the other side of the world. Now I live in the city because my clients are mostly foreign businessmen in a hurry. They fly in first class, grab a limo to the city, and never see anything beyond the local office and their hotel.

The silence doesn't get any more comfortable during the half hour train ride into the city. Marge holds William's hand, trying to comfort him. Or maybe herself. I can tell she's worried too. *It's all my fault; it's all my fault.* The refrain pushes at my conscience, urges a confession. I can't. I won't. If William learns what really happened, it'll be a full-time job keeping him from getting himself killed. I won't be able to finish April's ransom.

By the time we trudge the several blocks to my building, it's apparent the jet lag is catching up with them. Marge stumbles; I reach out to steady her. William glares at me because he was too tired to help her. Why did I want them to stay with me again?

The elevator in my building stinks worse than any of my roommate's herbal concoctions. The building management decided the elevator should be carpeted. The humidity and high foot traffic ensures that stepping into the metal box feels like breathing through yesterday's socks. To make things worse, the door sensor is finicky. Sometimes it thinks the doors are closed when they're open, and it will start moving before you get off. Sometimes it thinks the doors are open when they're closed, and it refuses to move until you kick the door just right. It's especially fun when it decides to open the doors when you're between floors. The longtime residents learned the trick years ago. I just kick where the biggest dents are.

I clear my throat and kick the door to get us going. William visibly bites his tongue. Luckily, the mechanical beast stays in place until all three of us get off on my floor. Tom is just leaving the apartment with a duffel bag slung over his shoulder.

"Hey, roomie," he says. "Thanks for the cash. I don't mind moving out for the week."

I wanted William to think my roommate was a professional – maybe a lawyer or a manager in one of the gleaming office buildings. The kind of roommate relationship you'd expect for an adult. "Tom, meet my brother and his wife," I say.

They exchange introductions and handshakes, William's terse and perfunctory, Marge's warm and friendly.

"Someone slipped an envelope under the door with your name," Tom says. "It had a note on it. Something about April? I left it on the kitchen table for you."

The daily picture of April I demanded as continuing proof of life. I thought they'd use the mailbox.

William drops his bag and trips over me in his rush to get to the door. I can't let him see the picture. I can think of a story to cover this as long as he doesn't see the picture. For a second, I'm absurdly reminded of how my brother and I used to race for the first brownie cut from the pan. It didn't matter how many brownies there were. What mattered was who got the first one. Anything else tasted bitter.

My brother wins. A jet-lagged Goody Two-shoes beats a recovering alcoholic on three hours of sleep, I guess.

His face turns seven different shades of red. He shakes the photo in my face, too quickly for me to catch anything but a blurred image of April with purple bruises.

"An interview for her thesis?" he yells.

The whole building must be able to hear him. "I can explain, if you'll calm down."

Bags fall over each other behind me. It's Marge at the door, dropping all the luggage we left behind. She runs over to us and grabs the photo from William's hand.

At her first glance, she nearly crumples. She catches herself against the fridge, one hand covering her mouth. A low moan escapes anyway. "April," she whispers. She's not speaking to anyone; it's a mother's call to her child.

When she looks up at me, her eyes are hard as flint. "William, shut the door."

William, surprisingly, obeys. No one else gets to order him around.

"Now, explain." She slaps the photo down on the table. "Explain why you've been lying to us for two days."

I'm used to disappointing William. Marge is a different story entirely.

I run a hand through my hair. God, I could use a drink. But not with William watching. "I was asked to do a job. I said no. They kidnapped April to force the issue."

"That doesn't explain why you lied," William says. "Or how they knew about April in the first place."

"I'm handling it." It sounded less ridiculous in my head. "I'll do the job and get April out."

"That's your plan? That's it? Whatever your little business is here, it obviously involves less-than-trustworthy people. How do you know they won't threaten April next time you need a little *motivation*?"

"We'll make sure April, and you two, are out of harm's way before I give them what they want. Once you're back in the States, you don't need to worry." *Please don't ask why.* If I tell William they're going to kill me, it'll look like I'm asking for their sympathy. I imagine both William and I agree that April's life is worth more than mine.

"You'll understand if I don't believe you," he says.

Marge's expression is just as unforgiving.

I take a step back, but the burn of their anger is just as intense. "I turned down the job because it was a dead-end." Running from Hong Kong was never an option. Whitney made it clear that my sudden absence, without a death certificate, would be considered grounds for prosecuting my brother.

My meaning slowly dawns on them. I spare them the effort of finding the right thing to say. "Right now, I just need you to stay quiet so the kidnappers don't get spooked."

Marge's face hardens again. "Absolutely not."

"We're going to the police," William says. "You used to tell us stories all the time about people who tried to handle things on their own."

I'm surprised he remembers. "They won't take the case seriously." I was hoping I wouldn't have to explain how April got involved.

"A foreign graduate student kidnapped by lowlifes won't get priority?"

"Yeah, here's the thing."

They look between each other, confused, waiting.

I clear my throat. "April . . . helped me out a couple of times."

"You turned my daughter into a criminal?" William's face is turning red again.

"No, no . . . just some minor bodyguard stuff." I take a step back, because I know what's coming next. "That's how the kidnappers knew about April. She helped me scare one of them off." Might as well get all the painful revelations out of the way now. Like tearing off a Band-Aid.

William launches himself at me. I back into the living room and trip over the pile of luggage at the front door. His knees land on my collarbones with a painful thump. It reminds me of the first time he got big enough to fight me. When I knew I was no longer the big brother he adored anymore. His first punch connects solidly with the side of my nose. It makes a sound like a cereal box being crushed. Warm, thick blood flows out of my nostrils. I leave my arms limp at my sides. Dimly, in the background, I can hear Marge yelling for him to stop.

I haven't been able to defend myself since I fought Mack. That's why I asked for April's help. When Mack figured out I was sent to get his confession on tape, he shoved a gun in my stomach. I managed to turn his weapon enough to shoot him in the leg. He spent his last breath cursing me. I can still remember the pinch in my gut as the hammer slammed back. The attorney general would later tell me I fought Mack for exactly one minute and forty-eight seconds, as long as it took for the cops listening to the wire to run into the warehouse.

It seemed longer.

It was the most bitter, most vicious fight I ever had. Long after I lost my respect for Mack, I remained loyal to him. He was, after all, my partner. I suppose he was a bad man; I wasn't in much of a position to judge. I couldn't resist my desires either. I only had a few affairs compared to his fifty or so, but then he had more opportunities. Even at my fittest, I never cut as dashing a figure as Mack did.

That's why I don't fight back when my brother punches the other side of my nose. I killed Mack, and I'll never forgive myself for it. It doesn't matter that he was going to kill me. It doesn't matter that the trouble started with him and his mob keepers. Mack was family.

The stars in my vision clear, and I see Marge with her hand on William's shoulder, trying to pull him back. William balls his fists, shakes them at me. "What's the matter with you? You're just going to lie there?"

He won't understand. There's no use trying. The only sounds are William's rapid, panting breaths. Too much time spent behind a desk has weakened his physique. When he worked with his hands, he could sling one bag of concrete over each shoulder easy. He rolls off me, frustrated, then channels his anger into kicking the suitcases.

"Will, stop," Marge says. "You'll hurt your foot."

He looks at her, as if asking what he should beat up instead. I'm not even good enough to be his punching bag.

When he finally calms down, Marge digs in her carry-on and pulls out two tampons. "It's not dignified, I know, but they're good for nosebleeds."

Dignity hasn't been my strong suit for a while. She gently inserts one in each nostril, then helps me up. It hurts, but it does stop the waterfall of blood down my chin.

"Let me see the picture." I sound like I have a bad cold. Or two tampons up my nose.

William stomps over to the table and back. "Makes sense that she's flicking you off."

It's true; she's giving me the middle finger with both hands that are holding up the newspaper.

"She's so bruised up." Marge's tone hovers near a sob. "Do you think they—"

"She has black belts in three different martial arts," I say gently. "I'm sure it's just from when they captured her."

"That's my girl," says William softly. "Why are they sending you photos if you already knew she was taken?"

My clown-like tone isn't helping me project authority. I pull the cotton out of my nose, wincing. Luckily, the bleeding has stopped. "I told them to send a photo daily. To keep them honest." The photo isn't easy to look at. She has a bruised cheek and a black eye. The fingers so prominently displayed are scabbed in places. It simultaneously breaks my heart and makes me proud. The accusations inherent in the gesture sting. While I'm planning all the ways I'm going to hurt Tiny after April is safe, my pinched tears magnify the headlines over April's middle fingers.

"Bad Luck for Seow"

"Another Real Estate Bubble?"

I wipe my eyes, not caring that William sees, and look closer. Not the full headline. Two sets of words. "Bad luck" and "real estate."

It was stupid of me not to notice right away. The way she is holding the newspaper is awkward, deliberate. The headlines she chose are along the header, previews of what's inside other sections. "She isn't flicking me off. She's sending me a message."

"Isn't flicking you off sending you a message?"

I carry the photo over to Marge and William; the three of us lean over it. "She's pointing to clues about where she is. Bad luck real estate."

William looks at me blankly; Marge looks hopeful but just as clueless.

"There's a lot of superstition here still. Especially in the real estate market. If a property is the site of a violent death, it's considered hongza, a calamity house. Just being listed as a hongza can drop the price of an apartment by 70 percent." I wait for them to follow my train of thought. "Calamity house, bad luck house."

"Bad luck real estate," Marge says.

"She's telling us she's being held on one of the hongza list properties."

William crosses his arms, reluctant to give me any

credit. "How many of these bad luck apartments are there? There must be lots, and not just in Hong Kong city." He's right.

I study the photo again. "I think she's still in the city." He's not convinced.

"No, look." I stab my finger at where an advertising flier hanging out of the paper. It's only a corner of the ad, but the image is all over the city. "This is the logo for Hong Kong eTransport. They only operate buses in this area."

"How are you going to narrow down the list?"

Excellent question. "The easiest hiding place for them is a place H—" Best not to give William any details that might let him go sniffing around without me. "They're probably using a property they own. That means commercial real estate. Big buildings, not single apartments or houses. I'll do some research, find a real estate agent who can do a discreet search for us."

"We could do some research at the local library," Marge offers.

It takes an outsider to remind me of how funky the local real estate market is. "The listings aren't really public, and some of them are more accurate than others. Sometimes the address of a whole building will be listed, when really just one apartment is considered cursed. We need someone with local knowledge."

William blinks slowly. "You're telling me that in one of the largest real estate markets in the world it's possible to have your property drop in value by 70 percent because of a listing in a secret database that you can never correct?"

I nod.

"This is a fucked-up place." He paces between the couch and the grungy window. "Marge and I can go see the real estate agent. We can pretend we're relocating a business."

"It's too dangerous."

He's warming up to hit me again. "I can handle a couple of street punks."

"They're not street punks." William's only advantage in a fight is the strength of his temper, but I can't tell him that. "It would be dangerous for April if word got out we were looking. Dealing with the agent will be . . . delicate. I'll handle it."

"Then I'll . . ." He paces faster, circling the tiny apartment so fast it makes me dizzy. "I'll call up one of your old friends in the Philadelphia PD, send them the picture. Maybe they can find some more clues."

I don't have any friends left in the department. Turning on a fellow cop is bad enough; turning on your own partner makes you the worse sort of rat. "We can't involve anyone else. I'm sorry. That's why I lied to you, there's nothing you can do."

Marge pulls herself up to her full height and grips my arm. She's six inches shorter than I am, but the look in her eyes makes it seem otherwise. "Of course there's something we can do."

"Look, I know you want a different answer, but I don't have one."

"Our daughter has been kidnapped." Her voice is as soft as a blade in moonlight. "We need *to do something.*"

I thought my experience as a cop would prepare me for this. I never thought much about what families went through after all the uniforms left. I never considered what it would be like to be the person who cared the most but could do the least. "You did some creative writing in college right?"

Confusion creases her face. "You want me to write a story?"

"April's ransom is five fake background checks. I've nearly finished one, but you could help me with the stories for the others. Then I can work on getting the supporting documentation."

"Are you sure they'll trade her for the work?"

Hostage exchanges are always tricky. I wonder how much I should tell them. "Let's just keep our options open."

CHAPTER 11

Dan
Philadelphia, 1991

THE MAÎTRE D' at La Pêche was too well-bred to let his disdain for my off-the-rack suit show on his face for long. For my third anniversary with Carol, I had gone for the tried-and-true formula, flowers delivered at her work and dinner at a nice restaurant.

I was already striking out. They didn't say it was a black-tie place when I made the reservations. We were both underdressed. I could already see Carol's accusations in her pursed lips, the same complaints that formed the refrain in all our arguments. *You dress like a slob. Would it kill you to hang your coat up when you come in? I'm not your mother. You don't plan; you don't think far enough ahead. Running late again? Is work all that matters to you?* The order of the warm-up varied, but her last words were always the same. *Maybe if you drank less, you could get your act together.*

We were seated at a table right next to the kitchen's

swinging door. Even I knew that was a slap in the face. The door hit the back of my chair regularly. The food, at least, I could look forward to. The whole restaurant smelled like butter and cream. The white tablecloth gleamed. Its thread count was higher than our sheets.

Our waiter, dressed in a black shirt and pants and a long, bleached-white apron, looked down his nose at us as he asked for our drink orders. I wondered if haughty servers made more than city cops.

I forced a smile to make up for Carol's lack of one. "It's our anniversary; I think wine is in order."

Carol sniffed her disapproval. I was surprised, though I guess I shouldn't have been. I had thought her complaints only extended to the nights I spend emptying the beer fridge in my workshop. Silly me.

"Maybe just waters," I mumbled.

The maître d' appeared at our table soon after. I expected he had thought of a reason he could kick us out.

"A Mr. Danson has called for you." He smoothed the lapels of his suit. "Would you like to speak to him?"

The warrant. The chief had threatened to call a judge at home to get it signed. I was hoping it was a bluff. I sighed and nodded, following the maître d' to a wooden counter near the entrance. He gestured to a phone that was sitting off the hook.

"It's my anniversary," I said in greeting. "My fucking anniversary."

I swear I heard Mack grin. "Comes with the job, part-ner. Donatelli's been ahead of every other warrant we've served. Chief pulled me out of my kid's Christmas concert to nail this one."

"Will a couple of hours really make a difference?" I asked, knowing the answer.

"I'll do you a favor and not tell anyone you said that." At my silence, Mack continued. "Look, I'm sorry. I know you guys are having . . . issues. I don't think this will take too long. I'll have you home in time for make-up sex."

I knew very well what I would come home to, my wife pretending to be asleep. At the time, I thought Mack was sugarcoating things. Serving a search warrant on a warehouse belonging to one of the biggest crime bosses in Boston wasn't a small endeavor. Looking back, I realize Mack knew exactly why it would be a short night.

What I knew in that moment was that if I wanted to stay on the detective track, I had to jump when the chief said jump. "Fine," I said.

"Meet you at the station in twenty."

Go fuck yourself. It wasn't fair to blame Mack. But it was easier than considering the tangle of problems between Carol and me.

I felt like I had failed Carol again, putting my work first. I walked back to our table hanging my head.

"Orders from the chief." I adjusted the neat napkin roll, still holding a gleaming fork and steak knife. "Our search warrant came through on the Donatelli case. Would you mind dropping me off at the station?"

Carol pushed her water glass away. "I should have expected this." She didn't seem disappointed; she just didn't want to let an opportunity to criticize me go to waste. In fact, she seemed a little relieved.

It stung more than I wanted to admit. She gave me a perfunctory kiss when she dropped me off, more for appearances than anything, I think. I imagined what the sex would have been like if our evening hadn't been interrupted, mechanical and dutiful, and felt a little relieved myself.

A flotilla of black and white was preparing to leave. Mack was already there. The chief noticed I was late. As the line of cars, lights and sirens blaring, descended on the streets near the warehouse, it occurred to me this was exactly the sort of scene that used to give me goosebumps. Me and my brothers in blue, defending the good citizens of our city against denizens of iniquity. Fighting crime like a caped crusader. Instead, I sulked in the passenger seat while Mack drove, eyes shifting nervously between the road and the bulletproof vests we both wore.

I thought Mack was nervous about a possible armed confrontation at the warehouse. We surrounded the building with tires screeching, red and blue light bathing the tan brick in alternating patterns. Then the order came to kill the sirens, leave the lights on. The lead detective, Neil Woodward, crouched behind the engine block of his car, megaphone in hand.

"This is the Philadelphia police. We are here to serve a search warrant . . ." I tuned out the rest, stuck on the coldness of Carol's goodbye kiss.

Mack nervously licked his lips.

We waited two minutes, then five, for any sign of life

from the warehouse. No one came out. No one shot at us. Neil put down the megaphone and picked up his radio. "M and M, you're with us," came the crackly call. Mack and I would be the first into the warehouse, along with the detectives.

A couple of uniforms gave us dirty looks. Being picked was an honor; it was an odd sort of lottery to win. Carol wouldn't miss me much, but I couldn't help thinking of Mack's four children. Wearing a bulletproof vest didn't mean you couldn't get killed.

We sauntered out of the car, Mack carrying the battering ram, like we did this every day. Like we weren't both sweating through our uniforms. He hit the front door of the warehouse once, twice. It rattled oddly on its hinges, like the lock was loose. The lead detective looked confused for a second, then motioned for us to back away. Gingerly, with only his arm extending into the doorway, Neil tried the door handle. It turned without resistance. He swung the door open, waiting for the hail of bullets.

Nothing.

"Well, let's clear it," Mack said. I mistook his confidence for bravado. The four of us, Neil and his partner, Mack and I, cleared the warehouse quickly. The main area was occupied by a resting forklift and a metal barrel. There were three smaller rooms—one office, one women's bathroom, one men's. The filing cabinet in the office had been emptied; the shredder was warm. Later, forensics would tell us even the bathrooms had been wiped clean of prints. The blackened remains in the barrel were just paper. They'd had time to shred and burn every piece of evidence.

The chief dressed the entire department down right then and there. Donatelli had known we were coming. We took too long getting ready at the station. Some of the backup uniforms were late. Someone must have said something over the radio. Someone had fucked up.

Mack kept his eyes on his shoes, as did everyone. We were quiet in the car leaving the scene too. I had sacrificed my anniversary for nothing. Two blocks from my house, Mack asked me for a favor.

"I don't feel like going home just yet," he said. "I need to decompress a little on my own, you know?"

Decompress was normally code for Mack and I going drinking at the local bar. But I certainly couldn't criticize anyone for drinking alone. "Sure, I get that."

He sighed, a little too artfully. "Leah will never understand."

I was ready to tell him where he could stick his concerns about his marriage, considering the night I just had.

"If she asks where I was, can you say the chief kept me late at the station?"

"Why would your wife call me?"

Mack brushed my question away. "You're right, she wouldn't. Maybe you should tell Carol. Carol and Leah talk. I just need a little time, that's all."

Carol wouldn't be talking to me. But I didn't mention that. "Sure. I'll tell Carol."

He drove away faster than I expected, like he had somewhere pressing to be. More important than a vague appointment to drink alone at the bar. I didn't go inside right away. I sat on the creaking porch swing to autopsy everything that had gone wrong with the night.

I thought about how I could have charmed Carol more. About how stupid I was to order wine when she'd been bothering me about my drinking. I thought about how I should be more like Mack, first to arrive at the scene, ready to charge into danger. A few years later, it became perfectly clear why Mack was so confident and why we never nailed Donatelli or anyone connected to him. Mack knew the building was empty. He was the one who tipped off Donatelli.

CHAPTER 12

Kevin
Washington, DC, 2023

ANOTHER INTERROGATION IN another tiny meeting room. Kevin knew the cramped quarters were intentional. Denton wanted the room to feel claustrophobic and airless.

"I'd like to discuss the informant you chose to work with," Denton said.

Kevin laughed. "Chose? Dan Mackenzie was the only lead we had."

"He was an alcoholic, corrupt police officer." Denton consulted his notes. "He fled the country because of his involvement in a bribery scheme."

Interesting. Kevin saw his first opening. "Your information is wrong."

Denton wouldn't be so easily rattled. "You want to make excuses for him because you were friends."

Kevin tilted his chair back and allowed himself a smile.

"Anyone who told you we were friends is definitely working you."

"He was an alcoholic." Denton flipped through pages on his laptop. "I have the medical records."

"That part is true." Kevin considered the possibilities. Denton's contact wanted Dan to be a villain. False accusations against Dan weren't necessary to make the case against Kevin. Someone wanted both Dan and Kevin disgraced. Someone who was angry at them both. "But Dan never took a bribe."

"According to you." Denton nodded curtly. "Let's move on. Clearly he was unreliable. Why work with him at all?"

"He was motivated," Kevin said.

"Because his niece had been kidnapped."

"Yes." Kevin deliberately kept his answers short so Denton would make his questions long. The more information Denton tried to use against him, the more Kevin would know about who was manipulating him.

"You also worked with Ryan Sing, aka Tiny Clint," Denton said.

"I did."

"Ryan Sing was the leader of the Little Caesar gang." Denton turned his laptop around to display a list of crimes. "Weapons smuggling, drug running, blood diamonds—he was involved in all of these things."

Even more interesting. "He was an enforcer, not a leader," Kevin said. "Ryan's job was to . . . motivate people . . . who weren't cooperating."

"You talk a lot about motivation," Denton said.

"It's important to understand someone's motivations,"

Kevin said, "For instance, why would someone want you to think Dan was a dirty cop and Ryan Sing was the leader of the Little Caesar gang?"

Denton snapped his laptop shut. But Kevin had already seen what he needed to see.

"My sources are reliable," Denton said.

"Are they?" Kevin asked. "How can you trust them if you don't know what motivates them?"

In a blink, Denton's carefully neutral mask slipped then returned. "You're trying to manipulate me. You have a reputation, you know."

Kevin shrugged. "I'm trying to help us both. My reputation will survive this." *Hopefully.* "But you don't want to be the investigator who was led on a witch hunt. No one will trust your instincts after that."

"I think we're done for today," Denton said. "I hope you are feeling more cooperative next time we meet."

Kevin whistled softly to himself as he walked to his car. He had struck a blow. But progress always came at a cost. Denton would go back to his sources and ask his questions. That would tip off the person trying to take down Kevin. And if Kevin was right, things would get worse before they would get better.

He dialed the number Saul had given him.

"You have something." Saul said.

"If you want to help, find out how Ryan Sing died," Kevin said. "I think he went to Thailand."

"If you're not sure where he went, how do you know he's dead?"

"Because it makes the story easier to sell."

CHAPTER 13

Dan
Hong Kong, 2015

FINDING A REAL estate agent with the right expertise and discretion to help me track down April will be a challenge. I don't have many friends in Hong Kong. On the rare occasion I feel like talking, my conversation partner is whoever is on the next bar stool. Never seeing them again is part of the charm. I'll have to settle for calling a frenemy instead.

Whitney answers. "Dan, I thought we m—"

I hear a rustling on the other end of the line, like the phone is being taken from her. "You have something for us," Jones says.

I try to relax the vise around my throat. "Just a tax fraud thing."

The line crackles again. "Nice of you to let me have my phone," Whitney says in the background. Then more clearly to me, "Let's hear it."

"I have a line on a depreciation scam."

The silence on the other end of the line isn't impressed. "It could be big."

She sighs. "Fine, tell me."

"I think one of my American clients is using the Hong Kong real estate market to hide profits."

Paper shuffles in the background. "Go on."

"If someone deliberately arranged to have a building listed as hongza so it would depreciate, that'd be tax fraud, right?"

"Yes." Her tone holds a glimmer of interest.

This part is tricky. I can't give her too many details or seem too eager to help. "That's all I heard. If you found a real estate agent you could trust, they could probably list some large commercial buildings that suddenly depreciated. A few hours of research on each and—"

"Thanks for the tip. I'll look into it." She doesn't even bother to sound sincere.

Good. That's exactly where I want her. "Maybe I could help. You know, as a peace offering. I could sit down with a real estate agent for you. It would have to be someone discreet; someone you trusted not to talk. If my client gets spooked, he'll wipe his tracks."

Something taps against the phone, a fingernail maybe or a pen. "That might be worth a little upstairs."

It'll be worth less when she figures out it's a wild goose chase. But I'll worry about that later. "I have some time today."

"I'll see if I can arrange it. Somewhere close to your apartment good?"

I try to keep the smile on my face out of my voice. "Sure."

A text arrives twenty minutes later from Whitney.

Lok Cha Tea House. Twenty minutes. Real estate agent will be in purple suit.

A response that fast is a bad sign; Whitney was rushing. That means she thinks, or Jones thinks, that my story is a ruse. The timing doesn't seem coincidental either. I'll have just enough time to get to the meeting if I leave now. I won't be able to arrive early and scout the location for listeners before I arrive. It's a safe bet Jones will be there.

I hail a cab and ask the driver to rush. A generous tip tempers his scowl. His near suicidal driving gets me there five minutes early. It'll have to do.

The tea shop is quiet, even though several tables are taken. Orchids in slender glass vases grace dark wood tables that gleam in the soft light. All the people I can see are too old to be government employees. One customer is hidden behind a newspaper, the only parts of him that are visible are his left hand and a pair of legs in a suit. The legs could belong to anyone. I burned Jones's right hand at the restaurant. It could be him. From a counter in the back, the hostess bows politely at me while she prepares a meticulously arranged tray of dan tat with flaky crusts. The egg custards are my favorite dessert here. They come in every possible flavor. I can smell the honey and ginger from across the room.

I'm getting looks for just standing like an oaf at the entrance. I take a table by the window. I need to figure out if the man hiding behind the paper is Jones. I don't want to reschedule, but Jones can't figure out which locations

I'm interested in. If he starts sniffing around, he'll get April killed. Think like a cop, I tell myself. How would I do surveillance in a situation like this? He couldn't know which table I'd choose. The answer is obvious. A directional mic, hidden behind the newspaper. If that is Jones. There's a way to know for sure.

I grab a used, empty teacup from the table next to me, ignoring the hostess's frown. I turn the volume on my phone up to max, then set an alarm to go off thirty seconds from now. The cup goes on its side aimed at the newspaper in the corner and the directional mic I suspect is behind it. I put my phone inside. The cup will focus the sound.

Twenty-three seconds later—I'm counting—a jangling of bells interrupts the hushed conversations at the tables around me. Newspaper man jumps a mile, swearing. I recognize Jones's voice. Everyone else gives me an annoyed look. Just then, a woman in a tailored purple suit carrying a briefcase enters the shop. My date.

I wave her over while Jones folds up his paper with crisp, angry movements. A spray of light brown liquid is splashed across his chest. Even better.

I tell the real estate agent I need a few minutes to catch up with my friend.

Jones's glare hasn't softened. "You're an asshole."

I take a seat at his table. "Yeah, I get that a lot."

"You're an asshole who's up to something."

"You're welcome to sit in if you're that interested." I hope he doesn't call my bluff. If Jones decides to sit with us, I'll have to waste everyone's time for the next half hour. And delay getting clues about April's location.

He picks at his wet shirt. "Then why the theatrics? This is the second time you've burned me in as many days."

"I don't appreciate being manipulated." My anger toward Tiny is getting the best of me; Jones is just a convenient scratching post.

"I don't appreciate being lied to."

"That seems unfortunate in your line of work."

"Maybe I will sit in on your little meeting." He's testing me.

I shrug. "If you want."

"You didn't seem interested in peace offerings at the restaurant."

"My temper gets away from me sometimes." Maybe a few nuggets of truth will make my lie more convincing. "Prosecuting my brother for tax fraud wouldn't just bankrupt the family; it would ruin his reputation. His business is everything to him. It's how he takes care of his family. He has a daughter you know, my niece April."

"The one who's here studying the economics of urbanization for her masters."

A chill straightens my spine. That's more than I expected him to know. "Seeing her father go through that would destroy her."

"So you're going to waste a week of your life researching real estate depreciation scams."

"Yep."

"For your niece, April."

"Yep."

He taps each finger in turn over the headline announcing

the imminent birth of a baby king penguin at Ocean Park. "Whitney says you have a good heart."

News to me. "I wouldn't know."

"I'm going to give you your little meeting," he says.

"Because I have a good heart?"

"Because I always find out what I want to know. Remember that."

I believe him. I try to shake off the chill he leaves in his wake. I have things to do.

The real estate agent is a plump Japanese woman poured into an eggplant suit that flatters her curves. There are nearly as many Japanese expats in Hong Kong as there are British. "Mr. Mackenzie, I presume." Her voice is soft without being deferent, the accent nearly undetectable. She hands me a business card, also decorated in purple, glancing at the door where Jones made his exit. She doesn't ask why Jones and I seemed anything but friends.

It occurs to me this whole thing could be a setup. Maybe she's an agent too. What did Jones say? *I always find out what I want to know.* Or maybe she's not an agent, but Jones plans to interview her later. I'll just have to tread carefully.

"Dan Mackenzie," I say. "Good to meet you."

"Aiko Kimura." She measures each syllable out carefully. I get the feeling she's studying me, but if I had just met a man who put his cell phone in a used teacup, I might be cautious too. "Whitney said you wanted to talk about hongza properties."

The hostess arrives with our tea. I give her the dirty cup and put my cell phone back in my pocket. Etiquette books never seem to cover the situations I find myself in. She pours tea into white ceramic bowls with practiced motions, bows, and leaves us. The scent of jasmine tea softens my shoulders, despite my nerves.

Aiko sips her tea, eyes closing briefly in pleasure. "Forgive me," she says. "So few places do tea right."

There's something about her demeanor that calms me, makes me want to trust her. I wonder if it's genuine or just the mark of a professional. Time to find out. "You know the market well?"

A crease appears in her forehead at my directness. "I wasn't aware there would be a quiz."

"It's important that I get this right." I let her think my motivation is making peace with Whitney.

She arches an eyebrow. "Well, let's get the interrogation out of the way then."

I realize I was hoping her reaction to be proof enough. It's not. "Are you part of an agency or do you work alone?"

"I work with Peak Real Estate Agency."

"They're swanky." I've seen signs with their name, all on places I could never hope to afford in my lifetime. The Peak is the local name for Victoria Peak, one of the biggest tourist traps near the city. "What kind of properties do you normally represent?"

"Mostly higher-end commercial transactions, like development projects or buildings changing hands. Occasionally, a residential or industrial project."

Those would be good qualifications for my query. Still, everything she's said so far could have been told to her in a ten-minute prep session before she rushed over here. I check her business card. It says "Peak Real Estate Agency" with a note she speaks Cantonese, English, and Japanese. I think back to an article I read in my roommate's paper when I was battling insomnia. "It's a hard time to be in the high-end property business."

She smiles again. "You're referring to the legislative measures taken in an attempt to control home prices in Hong Kong, like raising the minimum home payment, doubling the stamp duty on deals over two million, and levying extra taxes on foreign buyers."

All I remember was some news about realtors in street protests because they were going to lose their jobs. I raise my bowl of tea in a toast. "You win."

"Lovely. I do have other appointments today."

"I'm interested in properties where the whole building was listed as hongza, not just one apartment or unit."

"What about warehouses?" she asks.

It's a good thought, if not a pleasant one. I prefer to think of April being kept in some abandoned luxury housing instead of a dirty, echoing warehouse. Echoing. On the phone there was no sound of an echo, and no sounds in the background of the hum of activity surrounding Hu's operations. "Let's stick to commercial residential for now."

She looks up at the ceiling, thinking. "There aren't that many, maybe ten or twenty."

Inwardly, I sigh. That's a lot of properties to research. Except that I know from the anti-investigations I've done for Hu that he doesn't own any small commercial buildings. Not enough profit in it. "I think the scheme involves a large building, like one that has at least a hundred units. How many are like that?"

"In that case, only four or so."

That's better. "Tell me about those." I open to a blank page to take notes.

She pulls a laptop out of a leather briefcase, clicks a few keys, then lists an address that I know well. "This one is owned by a British company. They had five workers die in construction accidents before the inside of the building was completed. When the value of the building plummeted, the company that owned it went bankrupt, and it was abandoned."

I rule it out immediately. The only people responsible for security are the police that happen to be within earshot; it's a popular spot for underground parties. Even I've been inside. The first floor has no walls. The basement is the only floor with a ceiling. It's the floor you pass out on and hope no one assaults you in your sleep. I let Aiko finish her description of the property anyway. Even if she isn't an agent, I'm sure Jones will ask her which properties sparked my interest.

A few more clicks on her laptop brings up another listing. She turns the screen toward me. The picture shows several tall, white high-rises clustered together. The one she points out looks exactly like all the others. "This one is in Jardine's Lookout. It has two hundred units, but nearly half are empty. Six months ago, an entire family was killed in a robbery there. Rent is cheap for the area, but only Western expats will live there."

Jardine's Lookout is a fancy gated neighborhood that attracts anyone with enough money to afford it. The neighborhood would be an advantage for Hu. Security at the gate would make it easier for them to keep track of who's coming and going. I want to ask her if the remaining residents are clustered or scattered throughout the building, but that's the sort of question that would attract attention. The building is owned by a local developer, which is promising. Ironically, some of the safest buildings in Hong Kong are the ones owned by developers with criminal affiliations. Committing a violent crime in a luxury condo owned by the mob is like walking into Don Corleone's office and shredding his most expensive painting. I nod as she continues her description, keeping my face neutral.

"The next building is owned by the same developer," she says. "It's right next door. Several suicide deaths around the same time. But even expats won't live there. The whole place has been empty for months."

An empty building in a gated neighborhood. It'd be perfect. "Why won't expats live there?"

"The building has a rat problem. It started after all the residents left. With so much vacant space, it's hard to keep them out."

It's an odd story. They have exterminators in Hong Kong. If anything, chemicals lethal to mammals are more accessible here than in the US. "Seems like a professional could solve that problem."

She laughs. "Not these rats, if you believe the stories. You've seen *The Princess Bride*, right? It's a rodent of unusual size sort of problem."

That sort of story would be to Hu's benefit if he needed the space. I want to ask more, but I don't want to seem interested. "What's the fourth property?"

"A condo development owned by a Swiss company. Shoddy construction led to leaks in the gas pipes. No explosions thankfully, but several people suffocated to death. They've hired a Buddhist monk, a Hindu pandit, a Roman Catholic priest . . . someone from every religion in Hong Kong to come in and cleanse the place, but nothing's helped. Would they really do that if they wanted the building to remain labeled hongza?"

I'm distracted by the image of a parade of holy men visiting the glassy high-rise in the heart of downtown. Tiny wouldn't hide April there unless the Little Caesar gang has branched into registering companies in Switzerland.

"Mr. Mackenzie?"

I shake my head to clear it. "Sorry, you asked me something?"

"Why would they go to so much effort to cleanse the property?"

Right. I'm here investigating a real estate depreciation scam. "To throw investigators off," I say. "I mean, I'm not sure this property is involved, but I wouldn't rule it out."

"So, any likely suspects?" she asks.

Time to stall. "I think I need to go back to my source and ask a few more questions." I hold out my hand for her to shake, then realize she would probably prefer a bow.

She takes my hand politely.

"It was nice to meet you, Aiko. I'm sure Whitney will let you know if we need to meet again."

"Likewise, Mr. Mackenzie."

Once she's gone, I look over my notes and add any details I can remember. I don't trust April's life to my memory.

CHAPTER 14

Dan
Philadelphia, 2006

I DIDN'T HEAR my alarm because my wife kicked me out of the bedroom the night before. I had stumbled in drunk. Again. By that point, I was on my third wife, Ellen. I woke with a vague sense of dread normally reserved for mornings I was due at work. My breath could have killed a rat. While I was in the bathroom fumbling with the toothpaste, I remembered where I was supposed to be.

This afternoon was April's fifteenth birthday party. William had been planning it for months. I tried coffee first. When that didn't clear the woozy feeling, I took a shot of whiskey. I didn't yet know the phrase "functional alcoholic." Ellen was nowhere to be found. I didn't bother calling her cell phone. She was either already there, or she wasn't coming.

I jumped in the car, weaved my way over to my brother's house. I don't remember scraping my bumper along the line of cars near his driveway. I do remember how pretty the balloons were against an azure summer sky, floating lazily in the wind. Five balloons: white, yellow, green, blue, and red. One for each of the belts she had to go through to reach her first black belt. I remember how proud I was of my gift, a brand new dobok in honor of her achievement. The thick package clutched under my arm, I stumbled up the driveway toward the radio and people mingling I could hear in the backyard. William's party was a hit. A large crowd spread over the lawn, some piling their plates with food, some playing volleyball. April was standing near a table heaped with presents. I lurched in that direction.

A woman in a blue dress put her hand over her mouth. "Oh!"

Her stifled cry caught the attention of the people around her. The startled expressions, ranging from disgust to pity, rippled through the crowd until the entire lawn was staring at me. April's expression hurt the most. For a brief second, her face lit up. When she realized the state I was in, she frowned in disappointment. My breakfast of whiskey did a few cartwheels in my stomach. I managed to throw her present clear before I vomited into my brother's prized rose bushes. When I finally looked up, most of the guests had moved into the house. The first thing I noticed was how my present, the one I'd been so proud of, wasn't wrapped. I hadn't even taped the box shut. One sleeve of the uniform had spilled out onto the grass.

Marge leaned over me with a glass of water.

I shook my head. "I don't think I can keep it down."

She rubbed my shoulders. "To swish in your mouth then."

I did as she suggested. It only helped a little. I think it

was shame I was tasting. The back door slammed, and I knew William was coming.

"You shouldn't have come," he hissed. "Ellen called us and said you weren't coming." I could see from his posture he wanted to yell, but then all his guests would hear him airing the family's dirty laundry.

I sat back on my haunches, keeping my head low. Marge kept one arm under mine for support.

Behind him, I saw April fingering the white sleeve of her present. "It's exactly what I wanted," she said quietly.

"Oh, well that makes up for everything then," he snapped.

Marge dropped my arm. "There's no need to yell at your daughter."

William threw his hands up in the air. "Get him the—" He looked at his daughter. "Get him out of here. Now. I have guests to deal with."

The door opened again and a man in a Hawaiian shirt and beige shorts came out. He was wearing white socks and brown sandals. Then again, I was in no position to criticize anyone's appearance today. I looked down at my clothes. I hadn't changed since last night. Trickles of vomit darkened the knees of my wrinkled khakis.

The fashion disaster cleared his throat. "Will, I hate to mention it right now. I mean, I know you're . . ." He shuffled his feet; the lawn rustled. The toes of his socks were grass-stained. "It's just, it looks like there's been some damage to my car. And a couple others."

My brother swore under his breath. "Get the drunk's insurance card," he told Marge. "I'll get pictures. Then you're taking him home."

CHAPTER 15

Kevin
Washington, DC, 2023

"**DAN MACKENZIE, HOW** did you find him?" Denton asked.

Kevin was being interrogated in a new venue, Denton's office. The office was large, by government standards. Framed diplomas, awards, and commendations filled one wall. A clever flex, Kevin had to admit. Denton wanted Kevin to be intimidated by the display and relaxed by the more comfortable location. "Through an IRS contact," Kevin said. "He was an informant for them."

"Why did the IRS have someone working in Hong Kong?" Denton asked.

Kevin let the question linger. Denton's careful poker face flickered, his lower lip receding then reappearing. Kevin hid a smile. Denton wanted actual information now. Denton didn't trust his source anymore.

"Tax havens and undeclared foreign bank accounts," Kevin said. "The Foreign Account Tax Compliance Act had recently passed. US citizens are supposed to report foreign bank accounts they own, but before that law it was mostly on the honor system. After that law, most foreign banks were forced to tell the IRS if a US citizen had an account with them."

"So your contact, this IRS agent, was working on compliance with banks in Hong Kong," Denton said.

"Yeah, most of the time she was visiting banks to help them get into compliance so they could continue operating as normal. But she was also leaning on Dan Mackenzie for tips on US citizens dodging taxes."

"Why would Dan cooperate?" Denton asked. "He had the bribe money. He could have run. Was he trying to come back home?"

Still accusing him of all the wrong things. "Dan didn't take a bribe," Kevin said, "That was 'settlement' money forced on him by the senator's cleanup team. He didn't really have a choice."

"What senator?" Denton gestured with the pen he'd been using to take notes. "What do you mean Dan didn't have a choice?"

"Dan's brother had a business, Mackenzie Construction," Kevin said. "His business used the same accountant as Senator Holden."

More scribbling. More frustration evident on Denton's face. "You still haven't explained why Dan was cooperating."

Kevin bit back a retort. *Be nice. You have Denton where you want him, finally listening to you.* "I was trying to start from the beginning. So you can understand."

"So Dan's brother hired the same accountant as Senator Holden," Denton said. "Why is that important?"

"They didn't hire the same accountant by accident," Kevin said. "Holden invested his dirty money in Mackenzie Construction, with the condition that Mackenzie Construction hire his accountant."

Even Denton's scribbles were neat and organized. The handwriting was so good Kevin could clearly see the names and details from three feet away. *Senator Holden. William Mackenzie (brother), Mackenzie Construction.* "Senator Holden wanted his accountant in place at Mackenzie Construction so he could use the business to launder money."

Kevin nodded. "Senator Holden was Mayor Holden then, but that's the gist of it. Years later, when Dan turned on his own partner for also being connected with the mob, Holden was worried the scandal would eventually get back to him."

"You mentioned the senator's cleanup team," Denton said. "How did they force Dan to leave?"

"Dan had never taken bribes from the mob, his partner did," Kevin said. "But Dan had suspected and never said anything. The senator's team knew it was close enough that they could make it look like Dan was just as guilty. Dan would have gone to prison for what his partner did. So they offered Dan a 'settlement.' A bunch of cash in return for leaving the country."

Denton chewed on the end of his pen. "That explains why Dan was forced to leave. It doesn't explain why he stayed in Hong Kong to be an IRS informant."

"Dan wanted to protect his brother's family." When Kevin had started his career, he had been able to neatly divide people into good and bad. The more operations he worked, the more the lines blurred. Now he divided people into different categories: useful or not useful. "Dan's brother, William, had hired a mob accountant. But William hadn't known that at the time. When William finally figured out something was wrong, he fired the accountant and kept the books right going forward. But he never reported his accountant's crimes."

Denton was chewing on his pen again. Kevin was oddly satisfied seeing the scarred pen, an imperfection in the otherwise meticulously organized office.

"William became complicit," Denton said.

Kevin nodded. "Yes, exactly."

"Just to confirm my understanding," Denton said. "Dan Mackenzie had to leave the United States, or he was going to be prosecuted for his partner's crimes. And he was forced to stay in Hong Kong as an informant, or the IRS would have gone after his brother's business."

William Mackenzie had unknowingly participated in organized crime and hadn't owned up to it. Dan Mackenzie had looked the other way too. But both men had been willing to sacrifice everything to protect family. Good or bad?

"You asked why work with Dan Mackenzie," Kevin said. "Dan was useful, despite all his flaws."

CHAPTER 16

Dan
Hong Kong, 2015

WHEN I GET back to my apartment, it's nearly dinner time. William must have heard my keys; I nearly hit him with the door when I enter.

"Did you find out where they're keeping her?" he demands.

If only it were that simple. William, and nearly every other civilian I've dealt with, thinks that all cases run like an episode of *Law & Order*. "I have a good lead to research."

"Please, don't share any details with me. I'm only her father."

I open my mouth, figure out I don't know what to say, then shut it. William stomps off toward my room. I follow, hoping something brilliant will occur to me. It's true, he deserves more than the polite, formulaic responses detectives give to families. But I don't trust William not to try "investigating" on his own. I can't give him any useful details.

In my room, I find William throwing clothes in a laundry basket. Of course, they're sleeping here. I should have cleaned up. He pauses, watching a trail of ants climb up a wrinkled shirt into the mouth of the orange vodka bottle and back to the small gap between the baseboard and the wall. They're dining on the sugar patches left by the evaporated liquor. It could be my imagination, but some of them seem a little unsteady on their six legs.

"You seriously live like this?" he asks.

His eyes note each one of my housekeeping faults. The walls in need of washing. The wrinkled arm of a dress shirt hanging out of a drawer. Food wrappers overflowing from a trash can. The ants are a new touch. But I don't want to start an argument. "I meant to clean up. Where's Marge?"

"She went to buy food. You don't seem to keep any in the house."

Another thing I should have thought of. "You two really shouldn't be seen outside. From now on, just let me know what you need."

My brother gives me a familiar glare. "Food. We need dinner. Anything you'd care to share about your little meeting?"

I think through the information Aiko gave me, try to pick out a morsel that's safe to share. "She gave me four locations to research. I need to look at property records to see which ones are tied to Tiny's gang."

"Tiny?"

Shit. "I can do that research while I do the laundry."

"I can't be seen in the laundry room?" he asks with a

sneer. He heaps more clothes into the basket, wrinkling his nose.

Funny how I didn't notice the smell until my brother was here. "The machines are all labeled in Chinese. You could clean the kitchen and pick up the dirty dishes, if you want." I shake the ants free from the vodka bottle. "Rinse this out before you drop it in the recycling, otherwise the ants will find it again."

"I'm going to pour out any other bottles I find." He won't find anything in a bottle. I finished everything but my roommate's swill already.

"Leave the beer."

He shakes his head. "Someone should have cut you off a long time ago."

"You don't want me quitting now." I dig through the closet and find a box of laundry detergent, half spilled, in the corner.

My brother grips my arm in a vise, strong from desperation. "I won't let you fuck this up."

I stare into the dark void of the closet, remembering the headache that felt like an ice pick through my forehead. "I'm a functional alcoholic. I can't shoot straight sober." Every time I think I'm beyond shame, I surprise myself. "I don't have time to go through withdrawal symptoms right now."

His hand leaves a red mark when he releases me. "That's just great. Just fucking great. My daughter's best chance is a—"

"Pathetic, washed-up, sorry excuse for a human being?"

William may not be helpful, but he's not wrong.

"If only Mack could see you now."

That stings. I'm tempted to tell him who Mack really was, but I should keep my mouth shut. William knowing won't change anything. I take a deep breath, waiting for the anger to pass. Instead, the feeling intensifies. Red tinges my vision. "This is Mack's fault as much as it's mine."

"You can't blame your problems on a dead man."

All the bitter charges I have against Mack fill my mouth like venom. That I lied for him to cover up his affairs. That he started my career as an alcoholic. That he stole my brother's respect, when a crooked cop didn't deserve it any more than a drunk cop did. And William, acting all high and mighty? He must have an inkling of what happened inside his company. Of why his accountant left suddenly, leaving William to face an IRS audit and criminal investigation. This time, swallowing the words might kill me. "You want to know why I never left Hong Kong? Why I live *like this*. I can't leave. The IRS field office found me. Did you ever wonder why the IRS decided not to press charges?"

William shakes his head stubbornly. "What does the IRS have to do with Mack?"

"Mack's friend, your accountant, the one who was using your construction company to launder the mob's money."

He sinks down to the bed, rumples the sheets in clenched hands. "I don't know anything about that." His words lack the normal bravado. He's lying. William is never shy when he thinks he's right.

"Your accountant disappeared overnight. You're telling me you never looked at the books when you were cleaning up his mess?"

William rolls his lips closed, doesn't look up from the

floor. "I found . . . things. The IRS dropped it. I decided it was better not to ask. Our new accountant keeps clean books. I make sure of that."

"The IRS didn't close your case. I made a deal. I feed them tips on tax dodgers here, and in return, they leave you alone. I stay here to protect you."

He shakes his head; I can tell he doesn't believe me.

"And your sainted Mack? You want to know what Mack did on the nights he wasn't playing family man?"

At this, William looks up, eyes flashing. "Mack didn't know the accountant he referred was shady. He wouldn't do that to me."

"Mack was in on the deal. He was getting bribes from the mob for tipping them off. You laundered his money too."

"You're just angry that Mack accomplished everything you couldn't. He kept his marriage together. He was about to get promoted to lieutenant."

I laugh more harshly than I should. "Is that what he told you? I kept his marriage together because I lied for him. Mack's favorite hotel was that dive near Brewerytown. He'd pick up women in the local bar, then take them to the cheapest bed he could find. Sometimes he was at that hotel two times a week. If the relationship lasted more than one night, they skipped the bar."

"He wouldn't do that." William's standing now, ready to punch me again.

"That's how the mob got him. It starts like that, a few incriminating pictures. One small favor, and then another.

You remember the big Donatelli case? The one Mack and I spent years on and never even got one arrest."

William nods cautiously. Everyone in Philly knows about the case. *The Philadelphia Inquirer* even ran a series of articles on police incompetence.

"Mack tipped off Donatelli every time we were about to serve a warrant. He never would have made lieutenant. Every big case we landed, he got paid to sabotage."

I should slow down, find a way to tell him gently about Mack's death. I can't. I've been carrying around this poison for too long. "Mack didn't die in a shoot-out with a gang member. That's just how the department whitewashed the story. I shot him."

William shakes his head, forcefully this time. "No. That doesn't make sense. You wouldn't . . ."

"I shot him because he was going to kill me. I was wearing a wire. I got Mack to admit he'd been tipping off Donatelli."

"You betrayed him." The words are nearly whispered.

"I had no choice." God, I want my brother to believe me. To forgive me. Mack's ghost never will. "I was hauled into an interrogation room just like any other piece of trash we bring in. They had to blame someone. They had to convict someone. So I could help them get Mack, or I could take the blame for everything he'd done."

William sits down on the bed again, shoves his hands underneath his legs. "I didn't know. I didn't know about any of that."

"We're not even to the best part yet. Your friend, Senator Holden, heard that the department was going to use Mack's death to prove they had cleaned house. He had just won his first term. He couldn't take the chance that someone would connect Mack's death with the accountant they shared and your company. So he twisted arms at the department, changed the deal."

His eyes are glued to the carpet. He won't look at me.

"The recording was destroyed. I was the only piece of evidence left. I could accept the cash they offered, leave the country, and never come back. Or I could rot in jail like he should have." The last sentence surprises me. I never considered turning him in when we were partners. I crouch, so my brother is forced to see me. "I didn't run away. I was forced out. And I've been protecting you, the best I can, ever since."

He takes a few shaky breaths. A minute passes, maybe more, with him slumped over, frozen in place. "None of that changes a goddamn thing. If April dies, it's on you." He brushes past me. In the kitchen, I hear the sink turn on and dishes clatter.

The heavy laundry basket reminds me I have things to do. I find Marge's notes for the background stories in the living room, then make my escape to the laundry room in the basement with my laptop.

The humid air smells like a hodgepodge of competing detergents: lavender, lemon, spring rain, green tea, and grapefruit. The loud thumping of the dryer drowns out distracting thoughts left over from my argument with William.

I start with the research on the two properties in Jardine's Lookout. I needed Aiko's expertise to narrow down the field, but the final step requires information she doesn't have. Paper records routinely go missing from government offices here. I learned early on to keep copies of every scrap of evidence from every investigation. My laptop contains several hundred neatly ordered, encrypted directories. Several of these investigations were for the Little Caesar gang. I already know most of the shell corporations they use. The building with rodents of unusual size is owned by one of Hu's shell corporations. The rest of the buildings are owned by names I don't recognize. By the time the washer stops spinning, I'm sure April's in the abandoned building in Jardine's Lookout.

Getting into the building is a different matter entirely. A chorus of beeping tells me it's time to start another load. Every raid I went on as a police officer included niceties like backup and the best firepower the Philadelphia police department could offer. Gun laws in Hong Kong are strict. As a mere resident, I'm allowed a small handgun at home, but no ammunition. That has to be kept at the gun club where I practice.

My hands are dripping. I look down to see that my fingers are locked in tight fists around the wet clothes I'm transferring to the dryer, wringing the water out. Hu will have April under guard, at least three men. Three men in better shape who have better weapons than I do. Not good odds for April.

I remind myself I'm further along than yesterday. Yesterday, I didn't even know where she was. Today, all I have to do is figure out how to sneak into a gated community with an illicit weapon, disable April's guards, then get her, and my loudmouth brother and his wife out of the country before Tiny dismembers me. Progress.

CHAPTER 17

Dan
Philadelphia, 2009

I PRACTICED MY line in my head as the technician taped the microphone to my chest. *Mack, I have some information for Donatelli. To sell. Could you arrange it? I*—a sharp pinch on my chest cut the rehearsal short.

"Did I tear that tape off too fast?" the technician asked insincerely. "Sorry about that, I put the mic in the wrong place."

The lead detective, Neil Woodward, snickered. Just last week, Neil had been giving me advice on how to balance a detective job with a marriage. Neil was still on his first wife; she sometimes brought cookies into the station.

Patrick, Neil's partner, sipped his coffee. "Do a little of that on his back, would you? I think he could use it."

Funny how fast things turn.

When the technician finished, the small black knob of a microphone was nestled just above my appreciable gut.

I picked my shirt up from where they'd dropped it and somehow found the dexterity for the buttons. My torturer opened a black case and put on a pair of headphones, then nodded at Neil.

"Say something, Dan," Neil ordered.

I looked at him blankly. Say what? I'm sorry I didn't turn in Mack? I don't know if Neil would have turned in his partner either. Partners weren't supposed to do things like that.

"We need to test the microphone, asshole. Say something."

"Fuck you." I was tired. They had hauled me in three hours before our graveyard shift was scheduled, then kept me in interrogation for an hour. Satisfied that I was at best Mack's sidekick, they offered me a deal. Get Mack on tape confessing, and I would just be fired in disgrace instead of charged with conspiracy.

The technician's face remained neutral. "We're good, detective."

Neil slid my phone across the interrogation table. It stopped near a dent I know Neil put there with a suspect's head. Not that IA would ever hear about that.

Mack didn't answer my first call. Or my second. I knew better than to think he was sleeping. His current affair, Tara, was a nurse who worked the night shift. They always met if Mack and I worked the graveyard shift.

Finally, he answered on the third call. "What the fuck?" He was breathing hard.

I blanked. Neil shook his head, like he'd known I would fail, then shoved a notepad in my face with a line.

"I'm sorry," I mumbled into the phone. "I was at the bar and I overheard Neil and Patrick talking."

Cloth rustled in the background. Feet hit the floor. "Something on the Donatelli case?"

"Yeah. Something big is happening tonight."

"Tell me." Mack was, no doubt, counting up the money he would make by the end of the night.

"I want in this time." The initial sting of betrayal had worn off. I fell into my role, propelled by the inevitability of it all.

"Where can we talk?" Mack didn't sound suspicious, but he was smart enough to avoid making deals over the phone. Our conversation so far could be two detectives gossiping.

I paused like I had to think about it. "That warehouse where we found the dead junkie last week." IA had already set up surveillance there.

"One hour," he said. "Don't be late."

I drove myself to the warehouse to keep my cover. Mack's car was nowhere to be seen. But then, he was an old hat at this game. Despite the chilly night, my pants were stuck to my legs when I got out of the car. Gravel crunched underneath my sneakers and echoed in the parking lot. I looked around, not knowing exactly for what. Mob snipers? Mack hadn't sounded suspicious on the phone. But then, I hadn't picked up anything unusual in Neil's tone when he asked me to come in early.

I ducked under the yellow tape and pushed the door open. A dark, fetid smell assaulted me. It was the smell of neglect, human piss, rats, feces, and slime. The roof leaked.

I could feel the moisture under my feet. I told myself I paused to let my eyes adjust. Truth was, I considered running away. I wouldn't get far, I knew. But then Mack would know I at least tried. As I was trying to decide which was more of a coward's move, running or staying, Mack called to me.

"Back here," he said.

I followed the voice to a haphazard structure built of shipping pallets. Light from a weak moon filtered through a dirty window above our heads. A ratty old sleeping bag, nearly disintegrated, was balled up in the corner. Only our footsteps disturbed the slime on the concrete. Whoever called this home hadn't been here in a while.

"The smell's a little better here," Mack said.

He was right. A hole smashed in the window—by a rock or a bullet—allowed a small current of air. Still, I tried not to breathe too deeply. "I want 40 percent."

Mack smiled. He wasn't suspicious at that point. If anything, he seemed relieved. A partner with skin in the game made things less risky for him. "Twenty. Donatelli won't see you; he knows me."

It was a good start. But IA wanted an ironclad case. "Forty. Donatelli wants what I know, trust me."

Mack slapped me on the back. The sound echoed like a gunshot in the empty space. "Thirty. That's my final offer, partner." He meant partner in more ways than one.

Something tickled my chest, pulled softly at my chest hair. The tape on the wire was shifting. I wet my lips. "Thirty then. You can set up the meet with Donatelli?"

His eyes narrowed. "That's the second time you've used his name."

Shit. Play dumb. I looked around the warehouse, pretending to search the corners. "You think someone is here? I made sure Neil didn't see me leave the bar." I could feel the tape's tenuous grip with every breath I took.

"The warehouse is clear," he said. "I checked it before you got here. Tell me what you overheard."

I shook my head. "We tell him together. You just set up the meeting." A good criminal doesn't show his cards until he has to.

"You don't trust me?"

One strand of chest hair came out under the weight of the wire. The tickling sensation changed to a prickling. It occurred to me that may be the tech wanted it this way. "If I'm in, I'm all in." I had Mack's confession on tape. Now all I had to do was get out.

Mack nodded. "The money's good. You won't regret it."

If your conscience can handle it, I thought. "What was your last take?"

His eyes narrowed again, but not at what I said. He was staring at an odd shape beneath the fabric of my shirt. The prickling sensation was gone. The microphone was loose, swinging against the side of my gut, poking a round head against the cotton. "You son of a bitch," he growled. He reached for his gun.

My training kicked in. I knew I wouldn't beat him to the draw. His gun was halfway out of its holster already. I slammed my body weight into his midsection; we tumbled forward. The fragile configuration of pallets collapsed under our weight. I heard one shot, then the gun fell from his hand, bouncing down through layers of pallets. I wasn't hit; he didn't falter. I kept my arms locked around his chest, to keep him immobilized. Splinters lodged in my hands as we struggled. He was fitter than I was, but I weighed more.

The pallets tipped; he rolled me over. I felt his hand fumbling for my gun, even with his upper arms locked against his sides. I was counting the seconds. They would come to rescue me. Not because they liked me, but because they wanted my testimony to go with the tape.

His hand reached my gun. I let go of his arms and tried to pry my gun away. He stood up to get a better angle for the shot; I followed to keep the gun pinned between us. I wrapped my hand around the trigger guard, to block Mack's fingers. He forced me against the wall, clawing at my fingers. I could feel my strength giving way. Maybe they weren't coming to help me. Maybe they didn't care about the trial if we killed each other.

Mack angled the weapon toward me, kneed me in the gut, and stamped on my foot. I heard the bone in my big toe crack. The pain was blinding. My fingers slipped. I could fire the weapon myself, or he would do it for me. The sudden release of my fingers surprised him. I took the split second to turn the weapon into his hip and fire.

He stumbled back, tinging the swamp-like air with the rusty smell of his blood. I calculated the trail of the bullet from the entrance wound, just above his hip, and the exit wound, somewhere on the back of his leg. From the size of the dark puddle soaking his jeans, I knew I'd hit an artery.

"You son of a bitch," he spit the words like venom. Then weaker, falling to the floor. "You son of a bitch."

I was in interrogation for ten hours after I shot Mack. My familiarity with their methods didn't make the experience any less terrifying. Tell the story once. *I called Mack, told him to meet me at the warehouse. I told him that I had information for Donatelli I wanted to sell. Mack went along at first. Then one of the pieces of tape came loose, the wire slipped. Mack saw the outline against my shirt. He attacked me. I had to use my weapon in self-defense.* They interrupted me nearly every sentence. Did the tape really slip? Or did I make sure the wire was visible so Mack would try to kill me? Maybe I was crooked too. Maybe I wanted Mack dead so he couldn't turn against me.

Tell the story again, with more interruptions. See if the story changes. Make accusations until something sticks. Ask if I was drunk, say my memories were suspect. I remember the pair of them, veterans I would have once called friends, high on their power. They bantered between themselves, joked that I had probably sweated the wire loose. They made the room uncomfortably warm, then cold. They made me, the suspect, ask for water. Ask to use the bathroom. Then I had to tell the story again. I probably relived those ten minutes of my life a thousand times that day.

The person who trained me in interrogation described the process as half a boot camp. You break the suspect down, but you never build them back up. You make them unsure of their own name, then make them tell the story again. You pounce on any insecurity, mock them for it. At the end of it, I was shaking but my statement hadn't changed. They didn't have anything to charge me with.

Senator Holden's lawyers arrived with thick briefcases. I signed three papers that dismantled my entire life. The first was a document saying I knew I was being fired, and I would not sue the city for wrongful termination. The second was a document admitting I knew what Mack was doing, and failed in my duty to inform Internal Affairs. The third was a letter renouncing my US citizenship.

They made copies of everything for me, discreetly including a handwritten note with an account number at a bank in Hong Kong where I could collect my payoff. I didn't want the money, but I pretended I did. If I'd refused, they would have assumed I wasn't playing along.

My badge and gun had already been confiscated. I was led to my desk to gather any personal effects. The silence in the squad room was damning. At best, I was a cop who had turned on his partner. At worst, I was a dirty cop who had escaped punishment. I left the picture of my fourth wife on my desk. I took the picture of Carol, my first wife, I kept hidden in the top drawer. I knew I was moving, so I didn't bother to take anything else.

When I found the courage to lift my eyes from the floor, to show everyone I wasn't the monster they thought I was, everyone became studiously involved in work at their desks. I was prodded out the back and left next to the dumpsters in the parking lot.

Mack would have been happy.

CHAPTER 18

Dan
Hong Kong, 2015

I COUNT THE seconds by the tapping of William's pen. He's been staring at a contract on his open laptop on the kitchen table all morning. I don't think he's read a word. Every few minutes the pen stops, and I know to bend my head over my own work. I feel his glare without looking up. Marge is pretending to watch a badly dubbed movie on television with the sound kept very quiet. It's a low-budget romance, often interrupted by commercials with the dancing, cutesy graphics that are so popular here.

As the morning stretches on, their eyes flick to the door more often, waiting for the photo that will prove April is still alive. I know it won't arrive until after lunch, exactly twenty-four hours after the first photo. Tiny is punctual. The pen stops again; I stare at my screen, not needing to fake the concentration required. I rest my hand lightly on the mouse, making slight adjustments to the curve of the ornate text. It's a fake diploma for Yun-Fat Tsang. William's pen taps-taps-taps, jerking my fingers, distorting the text. This isn't working.

I close my laptop and shove the papers surrounding me into a pile. "I'm going out for more supplies." It's partially true. I don't have the expertise to fake a birth certificate or marriage license. I only know of one place that does work like that. It's a place Tiny told me about, a small copy shop tucked in near the Hong Kong University campus. I take the train out of the city center, grateful for the noisy, distracting press of the crowd. The passengers that get off with me are young, obsessed with papers and tests and disagreements with their roommates.

When I find the copy shop, it's busy with the legitimate business that provides a cover for their more profitable activities. Getting into the smaller room in back will require a few magic words.

I weave my way through the students at the large, beige copy machines and shelves crowded with school supplies. They eye me warily. It's obvious I'm not here for an assignment, and I don't look at all like a professor.

At the counter, there is a man the same age as most of the customers. His facial structure is Chinese, but his skin hints at a mixed heritage. Spikes of dark black hair are alternated with bright pink highlights.

"I need a custom order," I say.

His casual posture wavers as he studies me. He doesn't know me, and it's obvious from my Cantonese I'm not a local.

"Tiny Clint said you could help me."

"Depends on the job." He pulls a plastic sign from underneath the counter that says Back Soon! and motions for me to follow. Away from his post, his body language changes. The grace in his whip-thin body tells me he's dangerous.

He leads me down a short hallway with carpet worn thin. The hallway ends in a metal door meant to look cheap. I can tell it's not because of the lock. Smart criminals never use cheap locks. He opens it, waits for me to enter the dark space beyond, then shuts us both inside.

For a long second, it's pitch-black. I hope the sounds of his movement are him going for a light switch. Bright light floods the room, forcing me to blink. When I see what's on the shelves, I understand why they need good light. Above a desk on the wall, there is a very impressive collection of stamps. The kind of stamps used to fill out a fake passport. Tiny said this place could make you a citizen of anywhere, with any travel history you wanted.

"You're the ex-cop Tiny said was coming," the pink-haired boy says.

"Yes."

He stands with his arms hanging loose, but I don't mistake it for relaxation. The room is very quiet, like it's been soundproofed. "Convince me."

Somehow I doubt an official identity card means anything in a place like this. "What kind of proof would you like?"

"Name Tiny's favorite movie."

It has to be something with Clint Eastwood in it. If Tiny set up this loyalty test, he must have told me at some point.

I will my alcohol-soaked brain to recover the memory. Not *The Good, the Bad and the Ugly*. Tiny identifies more with the wrongly accused. "*Hang 'Em High*."

The punk nods slowly. "Tiny says to give you whatever you want, top quality. They'll pay me directly, and I'll even take care of delivery."

Tiny wants to make sure I can't take back my work. I should be glad I don't have to spend my own cash, but it means giving up one of my bargaining chips before we even meet to exchange April. I take the list of names, birth dates, and marriage details from my pocket. "I need these birth certificates and marriage licenses."

He scans the list quickly. "Easy enough." Without looking up, he pulls an envelope from the shelf. "Here."

"What is this?"

"Tiny left it for you. Said if you didn't come by today, I should let him know."

I suppress a shiver. Tiny's making sure my work stays on track, that I'm not distracting myself by doing something stupid like planning a rescue. By the stiff feel of its contents, I know it must be the photo of April. I was going to stake out the entrance of my building today, follow whoever delivered the photo. It's dark again suddenly. I grip the envelope tighter, as if it might disappear. A slant of light appears as the punk opens the door.

"Time to go," he says.

I carry the envelope and my disappointment out into the street. A wind has kicked up from the southwest. The already humid air gathers thickly in my lungs. A monsoon is on the way. I go into the next place with bathrooms, a busy McDonald's, to get some privacy. The photo is more heartbreaking than the first one. There's no hidden message to decipher. Just a sadness and exhaustion in her eyes that pours lead into my limbs. I stick the photo in my bag, hoping I can keep it dry until I get home to deliver the good and bad news.

CHAPTER 19

Dan
Hong Kong, 2009

MY FIRST ABODE was on the outskirts of Hong Kong, a studio apartment on the very edges of what could be considered the city. What attracted me to the place was the bar on the lower level of the building. Not one of those trendy places that had neon lights and fancy cocktails. This one had alternated between being a Chinese restaurant and a drinking establishment for most of its history. The carpet in my little slice of shithole still smelled like cream cheese puffs. When I was sober, which wasn't often, I would notice how the walls weren't plumb. If I set a beer down on the counter, the level tipped noticeably toward the street.

The bar below my first apartment is where I found Tiny. Or, I should say, Tiny found me.

I was drinking my usual, whatever the surly bartender chose to serve me. That's how it worked there. The bartender kept track of your tab, and the more you owed the worse your drinks tasted.

Tiny took the barstool next to me. It groaned in protest; he didn't notice. "Mr. Mackenzie?"

This happened quite often actually. A few weeks after I arrived, when my tab ran too high, I started my anti-private investigation business. Word had spread. Tiny didn't look much like the businessmen I normally worked for, but I didn't much care. Money was money. To be more precise, money was liquor and a place to drink it. I waited for Tiny to tell me what he wanted.

Instead, he flicked a finger at the bartender. The bartender poured me a whiskey, something dark and well-aged. I'd never been served anything this good before. He brought Tiny a water. Tiny watched me sip the whiskey, not speaking. I wondered if the whiskey was spiked, and I'd stumbled into one of those urban legends where I would wake up in a bathtub without my kidneys.

When I was halfway done with the glass, Tiny spoke again. I only recognized my name. At the time, I didn't speak Cantonese at all. Seeing my blank expression, Tiny tried again, this time in accented English. "My name is Tiny Clint. My boss wishes to speak with you."

I shrugged. "Good for him. I'm here anytime."

The bartender shook his head, muttered under his breath. Clearly, I was missing something.

Tiny smiled and drank his water. "You don't understand. You are new here. You will come with me."

My cop instincts, not completely gone, stopped my hand from lifting the whiskey to my lips again. I knew physical force was not an option. "Can I finish my drink?" I was just stalling, really, hoping for a brilliant idea. Or a distraction. Anything.

A tittering woman, already inebriated, tipped her way into the door, halfway supported by a friend. The friend batted her eyelashes at Tiny; he shook his head, contemptuous. "Just like my last girlfriend."

I pretended to take a sip, but only let the liquor touch my tongue. I needed all the coordination I could muster.

"They only see my muscles. They think I want to be their . . ." He searched for words. "Be their bodyguard." He rolls his eyes. "My last girlfriend used to flirt with other men just to start fights."

I must have looked a little shocked. Here was a man who was going to carry me off to God knows where, and he was confiding in me.

"Silly, right? I do my work and go out to relax and then she starts a fight."

I took another pretend sip. "I'm sorry to hear that. It must be lonely for you."

If he noticed my sarcasm, he gave no sign. "My next girlfriend won't be silly. She will be able to . . ." He searched for words again.

"Take care of herself?" I offered.

"Exactly."

I took another pretend sip. The room seemed steady. Maybe I'd sober up enough to figure a way out yet.

Tiny shook his head with another inscrutable smile. "It works better if you spill."

"What do you mean—"

"I mean, if you want me to think you're drinking, it works better if you spill. The level in your glass hasn't changed."

I looked at the short glass and realized my error. There was a design on it, a snake or dragon maybe, the scratches and fading made it hard to tell. It was easy to tell, however, that the amber line of the whiskey hadn't moved below the forked tongue of whatever it was. That's when I realized Tiny was more intelligent than most enforcers I know. I was outmatched on both fronts. "Are you going to kill me?"

Tiny shrugged. "I do what my boss says. But I doubt it."

The thought of defending myself made my stomach turn. I threw down the rest of the glass and accepted my fate. "Well, let's go then."

Tiny's car was sensible and nondescript, if a little larger than most on the road. I suppose a small car wasn't really an option. He asked me to keep my eyes shut. He explained, without apologizing, that if I didn't I would see our route and that would make his boss unhappy. It was oddly relaxing, giving in. I think I even slept a little.

I heard a large door rattle open, like the kind of door at a loading dock.

Tiny tapped me on the shoulder. "You can open your eyes now."

I was in a warehouse. A white powder floated in the air, forming an almost mist that hid the workers I could hear moving around me. There were large vases, the size of a young child, everywhere. Finished vases on shelves were being taken down, filled with plastic bags wrapped in black tape, then nestled in crates for shipping. Fired vases were lined up on tables waiting for designs from an assembly line of craftsmen and their precise brushstrokes. Heat emanated from a back room, a kiln I guessed. That I had been taken to a drug dealer's warehouse was a bad sign. That the drug dealer hadn't bothered to hide his activities from me was a worse one.

Tiny led me to a man whose bearing made him instantly recognizable as the boss. "This is Hu." He bowed slightly to his boss. "Dan does not speak Cantonese, you will have to use English."

What I noticed first was Hu's lizard eyes. Intelligent, cunning, and without mercy. "My business is going well, as you can see."

I nodded, afraid of how my voice would sound. Liquor never gave me courage, any more than anesthesia would.

"I understand you offer services that help businessmen protect their success."

I never really intended to get into the business of helping men like Hu. I would have been content to stick with white-collar criminals. But it was clear I had no choice. "I do."

"You will help me." It wasn't a question.

"I charge hourly." A different warehouse, but it felt just like the one I'd been in with Mack. I'd been carried away again, by forces outside my control. I knew nothing about this could end well. My only option was to do one job for Hu, then run. I was planning my quiet escape from Hong Kong when Whitney found me. Then, I couldn't even run.

CHAPTER 20

Dan
Hong Kong, 2015

I WAKE UP to the sound of William's stomping in the kitchen and a sore neck from the lumpy couch. At the small table Marge sits dead-eyed, nursing a cup of coffee. The table is set for three.

"Morning," I say to Marge. I don't greet William. It's too early for an argument.

I line up the tasks in my head: find fresh clothes, shave, shower, change. I have an appointment with Aiko today. I asked if she would take me around to the properties we discussed so I can examine them. I told Whitney I needed Aiko because I had more questions for her. The truth is, I need Aiko as cover when I go into Jardine's Lookout. If Tiny is expecting me at all, he'll be expecting me to arrive alone.

There's a basket at the end of the couch with my clean clothes. Someone's folded them neatly, probably Marge. Normally I wouldn't bother changing from what I slept in and wore yesterday, but I want to keep up appearances for my houseguests.

My bathroom is cluttered with the toiletries of three people and my mess. Marge's fruity shampoo, my brother's expensive shaving cream, and his straight razor. I search in the chaos for my cheap disposable. Shaving is another thing I don't normally bother with daily, but it's necessary for my business today. I'm sure the guard at Jardine's Lookout has been given a picture of me.

I use my brother's shaving cream and hope he notices. Without my normal scruffy beard, I look surprisingly respectable. Next, shower. I avoid my naked reflection in the mirror and step into the tub, noticing that it could use a cleaning too. My paunch mocks me more than usual today. It reminds me how unqualified I am for the job of rescuing April.

A clean pair of khakis and a button-down shirt completes my transformation into an honorable citizen; I nearly don't recognize myself. Someone who just might be able to make it into Jardine's Lookout if the rent-a-cop doesn't look too closely. A true disguise isn't an option without making Aiko suspicious.

The kitchen smells like fried eggs and butter. William lords over my rarely used stove, making eggs-in-a-basket. It's a buttered piece of bread with a circle cut in the center for the egg to cook inside. Mom always made them for us on lazy Sundays after church. The spatula pauses mid-flip as he looks up. "You look better today," he says grudgingly.

I hate that his approval matters to me.

"Bring your plate over," he says.

I wade through the nostalgia to cross the kitchen. He slides the sizzling, perfectly browned toast-egg combination onto my plate. For once, there is no contempt in his eyes. He reaches into the fridge, pulls out a cold beer, and hands it to me.

It's as close to an apology as I'm going to get.

Breakfast is uncomfortable, but quiet. The silence is a welcome change. I go back to my laptop as soon as I'm done. The Photoshop work on the diplomas is painstakingly slow. It's hard to keep the mouse steady with the chorus of what-ifs running through my head. What if I do have to exchange the ransom for April? Will Hu really let her go? Will he target her later if the work isn't good enough? What if I can't keep William out of the way? An image of the dead baby Mack and I found in the foreclosed house flashes through my head. I can still see the medical examiner's report. *Cause of death: hypothermia. Infant was likely dead when neighbor called to report noise disturbance.*

It's a little reminder I carry with me that sometimes the best intentions don't matter. Sometimes the best we can do isn't enough.

The day stretches by; we're all watching the clock. Today, I'm sure the picture isn't waiting for me with any of Tiny's friends. I don't have any reason to visit the copy shop again, and Tiny knows that. I won't be able to follow the delivery man, as I had hoped to yesterday, because I have the appointment with Aiko. I force my attention away from the frustrations of the day to my work. The diplomas. The transcripts. The stories Marge spun out of thin air, made real, that just might buy her daughter back.

William gives up trying to read contracts and busies himself cleaning the apartment. At least the bathroom will get scrubbed. Marge knits something, the needles clicking mindlessly. At 1:00 p.m., it's time to meet Aiko downstairs.

"Text me when the picture comes," I tell William. "The second it comes."

He nods dully as he scrubs plates too hard in the sink. I leave the two miserable parents behind and paste on a smile for Aiko.

Except for a different suit, she's exactly as she was in the restaurant, punctual and meticulously put together. Her car isn't fancy, but not a speck of dirt or wrapper is in sight. Her surprise at my appearance is encouraging. "You clean up well."

She navigates the hectic Hong Kong traffic with implacable grace, assertive without being aggressive. I'm only interested in the abandoned building in Jardine's Lookout, the property we're visiting last, but I have to feign interest in the rest of them to keep Jones off the scent. I wear out my head nodding. I make up questions, then forget what I asked before she answers. Finally, we leave Hong Kong proper and head toward the abandoned high-rise in Jardine's Lookout, where I think April's being held.

My pulse speeds up as the traffic thins out. I can see the entrance to the neighborhood now, complete with a small guard's station next to a tall gate. I know the guard will have my picture. Tiny wouldn't overlook that detail. My only advantage is the general laziness of most of the big-name security firms. It's the same here as everywhere. They give some inexperienced kid a uniform, a pair of cuffs, and a Taser, then pay him minimum wage to watch TV all day. If he likes the show, my newly polished appearance and unlikely companion may get me by.

As Aiko approaches the guard's station, I pretend to search for something in my bag. A sneaking glance at the guard tells me he's young, as expected, twenty at most. I hear a television in the background. I recognize the commercial for seaweed chips. Sometimes I buy them and pretend that ingesting seaweed sprinkled on fried potatoes means eating healthy.

Aiko explains she's a real estate agent, and she's here so her client can look at an apartment.

The guard glances around the interior of the car, at me. The overly dramatic chords of a soap opera signal the end of the commercial break. His attention flickers back toward the television. He looks at me again, but it's a token effort. The mild discomfort of his face advertises his thoughts. I could be the guy, but I do look a little different, and if he gets me out of the car he won't know who fathered the child.

He waves us on. I don't sit up until the guard's post is well behind us.

Aiko raises an eyebrow. "If you're going to use me, you could at least tell me why."

I'll have to make up something. "I—uh—had a bad night here once. Lost my temper with some cad who was bothering a friend of mine at a party." If I'm going to lie, I might as well make myself sound gallant. "They threw me out."

"Uh-huh," Aiko says.

"Really."

She shakes her head, then holds up a hand to keep me from speaking. "I can guess why you were thrown out, if you don't want to tell me." Because I was drunk, she means.

I swallow the insult, hoping that she won't mention the incident to Jones. She turns the car precisely through a maze of streets. I'm trying to keep track of our route on the map in my head when my phone buzzes. I glance at the clock on the car dashboard. It's probably William, texting me to say April's picture arrived. Texting me *late* just to rub salt in the wound.

The message on my phone stops my heart.

No picture.

I look at the clock again. It's ten minutes past two. Very late for the normally punctual Tiny.

The phone rings as I'm staring at the words. It's not my brother and it's not Tiny; the number is unknown. I answer, my mouth as dry as sawdust.

"Have you finished the ransom?" demands a rough male voice.

My brain spins, trying to identify the caller. He sounds vaguely familiar, one of Tiny's underlings. I think he broke my ribs once. "I said two weeks. It's only been three days."

Aiko looks away from the road for a second, studies me. She will definitely tell Jones about my phone call.

"You have one more day." The caller hangs up.

I look at William's text message again, as if it would change just because I wanted it to. No picture of April has arrived. The kidnappers have changed the timeline. This is bad. Very bad. It means the kidnappers want me to finish the ransom without proof that she's alive. She's either seriously injured or dead.

"Are you okay?" Aiko asks.

The car is stopped now. I should have noticed. We're in front of a tall, white building. Gleaming windows, most covered by curtains, give the illusion of habitation. The abandoned building where I think April is being held. "Yeah, fine. Can we drive around the block? I'd like to get a feel for the place."

What I really want to see is the security layout. Where the cameras are, where there might be blind spots, how many entrances and exits there are . . . anything that might help me break into the place. Which I'll have to do in the next ten minutes. I'm woefully underprepared. There's no time to pick the best escape route. I have no gun. And Aiko—I need to find some plausible reason for her to wait while I go in the building.

She circles the block obediently. I count the security cameras. Two on each corner, to cover both sides. No open windows. One emergency exit, held shut with a chain, and only one entrance. There's a dome camera by the entrance. Generally, that means the camera inside the dark hemisphere can only cover part of the area at any given time, but you can't tell where the camera is pointed.

"I'd like to see if I can get inside," I say.

Aiko's mouth falls open. "You want to break in? What could you hope to find?"

Both excellent points. "Sometimes they post a guard on these sorts of properties. There's no graffiti, no broken windows. Makes me think someone is keeping an eye on the place. I think I can talk my way in."

"But why?"

"To see about that rodent problem."

She doesn't look any less skeptical.

"If it's real, or a ruse the property owners are using to keep the value down." Time to leave before she thinks of more questions. "I'll be back in twenty minutes at most, I promise." Or dead. One of the two.

I turn the corner toward the entrance, to keep up appearances for Aiko. Once out of her view, I walk on by, in case someone is watching the front door camera. My entrance won't be stealthy, but there's no need to alert them before I have to. I scan the sidewalk for something—anything—I might use to break glass. My quick walk by the front door confirms there is no guard. It's the prominent signs and the obvious security cameras that are keeping this building in good condition.

There's nothing on the entrance side of the building. No planters. No workmen with a toolbox I could steal from. Nothing. I turn a corner again, now on the far side of the building from Aiko. Who has probably called Jones already. Not that it matters now.

The sidewalk is deserted of people and sparsely populated with things. A bench by the bus stop. A heavy ceramic pot with shriveled plants inside and a tray on the bottom, dirty with neglect. Guess they don't pay the gardener anymore. I'm about to turn the corner again, to test the security on the emergency exit, when I reconsider the base on the planter. It might separate, or at least I could break it off.

It's hard to keep from running as I retrace my steps. When I duck closer to the building, where the planter sits, I know I'm out of the sight of the cameras. My watchers may or may not notice the suspicious disappearance.

The planter is too heavy for me to tip, much less lift, when full. I shovel the dirt out with my bare hands, throwing handfuls on the ground. I don't bother to see if there are people on the street. It won't change my plans. When the planter is half-empty, I'm able to tip it over. The tray is fused to the bottom. It's still too heavy to lift and drop, but I might be able to break a piece off. The size of a brick would do. I tip the planter again, until it's upside down. The dirt, dried from neglect, stays cemented inside the pot. I shove the pot down, hear myself grunt, hoping the fall will damage the tray.

With a sharp crack, the edge of the tray splinters. A chunk the size of my fist separates. Good enough.

I might as well break the window in front of me. The noise will bring April's guards, no doubt, but there will be fewer cameras inside the rooms. There are sure to be cameras watching both lobbies.

The first hit with my ceramic weapon only nicks the window, but leaves my hand bleeding. In the reflection, I can see the street is still blessedly empty. A place where more people live than work. I hit the glass again, feel the sharp ceramic edges dig into my fresh wounds. Spider veins of blood down my arm echo the angular, radial lines that appear in front of me. Again. This time the glass shatters, but the hole is only a foot wide. I kick at the edges, expecting bullets to appear from the other side at any time.

It seems to take hours before I've widened the hole to something I can crawl through, but my watch tells me it's only been two minutes. Still, no guns waiting for me. I should be glad. I'm unsettled instead. If there are no guns, no people, maybe April's been moved.

I'm in an office, long unused. Dust has settled on every surface. Most of the useful equipment has been removed. Only the odd keyboard remains on any of the desks. Stacks of brochures with glossy photos fill the garbage cans. Must be the leasing office.

I don't see anything that would help me in my pursuit of April, not even a stapler, so I keep moving. The leasing office opens into the lobby. I see the cameras on the ceiling and run toward what looks like the elevators. Power is on in the building, I can hear the background whirring of the HVAC system. But the elevators are disabled and dark. The door to the stairwell is open. I pull up the pictures of April in my mind and examine the background. There was no natural light. The room was large. Dim. It's possible that they were taken in a windowless room upstairs, but the basement is more likely. And an easier place to hide.

I check my watch. Ten minutes since I left Aiko. Five since I broke in, and still no activity.

My suspicion is confirmed by the dim light in the stairwell to the basement. Several sets of footsteps disturb the dust on the stairs down, none go up. There are too many prints to count. Could be two men or ten.

The stairs lead to a utility room with the door propped open. The light is on. I tense. There are people here. I grab makeshift weapons from a toolbox as I pass, a hammer and a long screwdriver. There's no time to search for better ones.

From there, I find an elevator lobby and a large garage. A dirty arc on the carpet points toward the garage. I enter the large, echoing space cautiously. It's hard to walk quietly on the dirty concrete. Anyone can hear me; it's small comfort that I'll be able to hear them too. A slash of light escapes from a door nearly fifty yards away. It's a small room, tucked into the corner of a garage. A janitor's office maybe. No sounds of people yet.

I find myself running before I can think about it. By the time I get to the door, I'm panting. It's labeled "Maintenance" in three languages. I wait a second, maybe two, to see if anyone will burst out. No one comes. I throw open the door, ready to hit anything that moves with my meager weapons.

The room is lit, but empty. An upturned chair is near the back wall, with bits of rope thrown haphazardly on the dark carpet. The chair and the rope are useless, but that's where I find myself anyway. I squeeze the rope until the braids bite into my palm. Too late. I'm too fucking late. The flash of scarlet when I open my hand slaps me. How could I have missed that? Then I realize it's my own blood from the cuts on my hands. The puddle on the carpet isn't mine though. The blood pool is the length of my forearm and half again as wide. April's blood. It has to be.

I throw the chair across the room; it clatters against a row of water meters. Tiny was here. His goons were here. I was too slow, too stupid, and too weak.

She could still be alive, but she's definitely injured. I

press at the carpet, try to guess at the layers beneath. Blood pools on carpet can be tricky. Depending on the rate of flow and the amount of padding underneath, the size can be deceiving. Beneath me, I can only feel light padding. It's a faint hope. I'll leave out the details when I tell William. I'll just say I found where she was kept.

Scuffling sounds from the garage interrupt me. A voice in Cantonese yells, "Someone's in there!"

There must be at least two of them, or there'd be no need to say anything. I take another quick look around, but there are no immediate clues. I have to run. The men are only thirty yards away when I exit the room. I see the sign for another stairwell, closer than the one I used earlier.

My hunters are two of Hu's goons that I vaguely recognize. They have guns out, but aren't shooting. One has a buzz cut, and the other one has a shaved head. A sound from the corner distracts their attention. A hulking shadow of a man, escaping up the stairwell I came down. Tiny?

The goons pause, look between the stairwell door and me. I remind myself to run, let them figure it out. They'll shoot me if they want.

"You get him, I'll get Dan," Buzz Cut says.

Surprise makes me stumble. Hu's goons are chasing Tiny. What the hell happened here? Gun shots ring near my ankles. Buzz Cut is trying to disable me, not kill me.

I see a door for another stairwell and run. *Fuck.* I left the hammer in April's prison. The door slams behind me with Buzz Cut uncomfortably close behind. There's nothing I can use to block the door. A screwdriver is no match for a gun, especially when Buzz Cut gets tired of trying to take me alive.

There's a small gap between the stairwell door and the frame. Maybe enough. I stab the screwdriver into the space up to the handle. The door rattles but doesn't open. Buzz Cut pounds on the door. The door rattles again, the screwdriver slips a millimeter. Time to make my escape. My heart threatens to give out as I run up the stairs. This stairwell doesn't exit near the elevators on the main level. I remember the chain blocking the emergency exit and follow the signs to the lobby, mindful that Shaved Head is around somewhere too. I hear footsteps pounding out the front doors. Hopefully it's Tiny and Shaved Head.

I wait as long as I dare, then run. It's bright outside. And quiet. Surprisingly, eerily quiet except for the sound of an idling motor. Aiko. My ticket out. I wipe my bloody hand on the inside of my shirt. I don't want to delay our exit with any questions. That can wait until later. Twenty-one minutes since I left her. The first thing I got right today.

Aiko looks at me suspiciously. She might not be able to see my injuries, but even I can smell my sweat.

"Stories about the rats were true," I say.

She shakes her head and reaches for the shift handle, puts the car into drive. "I don't get paid enough for this."

A man starts pounding on the passenger door behind Aiko; I jump and Aiko screams. Through the flurry of fists, I can just make out Tiny. Around the corner, I can see the ankle of a prone man. Shaved Head, probably, taken down by the man who used to give him orders.

"Help! Let me in!" Tiny yells.

Aiko slams her foot on the accelerator and the car jumps away from the curb.

Instinct overrides my common sense. "No!"

She stops the car, nearly angled into traffic. "You know him?"

I try to process the evidence, confirm my gut feeling. The kidnappers moving up the timeline. Tiny was being chased by his own men, and now he wants my help. It could be a ruse to get close to me. Will I be putting Aiko in danger? There's no time to work through the logic. Buzz Cut will find his way out of the building any second now.

"Unlock the door," I say.

Tiny's staccato rhythm against the windows continues for a long second while she considers, then unlocks the doors. He jumps in and tries to scrunch himself so he can't be seen in the windows. In any other situation, it would be amusing. Aiko's eyes are narrowed, calculating. She should be afraid, surprised.

Instead, she drives away calmly. As if everything's normal.

Buzz Cut runs around the corner, gun drawn. I duck down myself, looking as ridiculous as Tiny. But from a block away and growing, where the seat blocks Buzz Cut's line of sight, maybe it will do. I peek in the side mirror, see him bringing a phone up to his ear. He's either reporting that he lost us or reading off Aiko's license plate.

Once we turn the corner, Tiny starts talking. Between his panic and the fact he's speaking mostly to the floor, I can barely make out every other word. Mostly, I'd like to beat him with a crowbar.

I settle for cutting him off. "You want our help getting out of here."

Tiny nods, then resumes his incomprehensible rant.

We're moving slowly, still on residential streets, where speeding will attract attention. I scan the sidewalks as we pass them, watching for any of Tiny's friends. Or ex-friends, I guess. "Why the fuck should I help you?"

My answer is a dull thud from the back seat. I whirl around, half-expecting to see Tiny shot. But there's no shattered window. Just Tiny, pounding his fist into the carpet, his words muffled by clenched teeth. "April . . . knife . . . escaped . . . my fault."

I think of the blood pool on the basement carpet, my silly hopes. "April was knifed."

He shakes his head, pounds his reddened knuckles into the floor again. "You're not listening."

"Then talk slower. To me, not to the floor."

"April escaped. We have to find her before they do. They'll kill her."

She's alive. I feel my gut unclench, then twist again. They? Tiny doesn't consider himself part of the gang anymore? And why would they kill April before the ransom is finished? "You haven't answered my question. Why the fuck should I help you when you're the one who kidnapped her?" I'd rather dump him on the corner and leave him to what he deserves.

The car stops. Aiko looks between us, trying to make a decision. That calculating expression is back on her face. Definitely a very special sort of real estate agent, which means Jones has been playing me from the beginning.

Tiny peeks his head above the door. "I know where she is. We have to go get her."

It's exactly what I want to hear, which means I can't trust him.

He risks sitting up, spreads his hands across the shoulders of my seat, shaking it. "You don't understand. You have to listen to me. April killed Hu's son. They don't care about the ransom anymore."

Shit. No father was prouder of his son than Hu. His son was the heir apparent of the entire criminal enterprise, perhaps the reason for its existence. It explains the odd phone call. They just want to get what they can out of me before I figure out they don't have April.

My first thought is to tell Aiko to drive as fast as she can. On my second thought, I remember that whatever Aiko's role in this is, I have no right to put her in further danger. "There's a way out of this neighborhood on foot, right?" Otherwise, there would be no way for April to get out.

Tiny, eyes still wild, nods.

"We'll leave that way. Aiko will go tell Jones what's happened. That we need his help."

Aiko feigns innocence. "Jones? I don't know—"

"Save it," I growl. "He sent you to find out what I wanted. Now you can tell him. His help in rescuing April, in return for my cooperation."

They both start talking at once, Aiko trying to convince me of her ignorance and Tiny insisting we just drive.

"Would you both shut up?" I have to yell to be heard. "We can't take on Hu's entire gang by ourselves. We need help. Aiko, if you want to pretend you have to ask Whitney who Jones is, fine. I don't care. Just tell him what I said."

She huffs. "I might as well drive you. Call him yourself and set up the meeting."

"After we get out in one piece. We need a way to hide Tiny."

Aiko looks at the hulking form in her back seat. "You're Tiny."

"Tiny Clint," he clarifies.

She raises her eyebrows. "Of course. There's a lever along the top that will fold down the seats. You can crawl into the trunk from there."

Tiny doesn't fit. Aiko keeps us moving in circles near the gate as he contorts himself, grunting and sweating. No matter how he arranges himself, either his head or his feet stick out.

The second time we pass the toy store, I have an idea.

"Give me all your cash," I tell Tiny.

He blinks sweat out of his eyes. "My cash?"

"You want to survive this? Give me all your cash." It feels like I'm mugging him. First fun I've had all day.

He rearranges himself so he can reach his wallet, then hands me a thick wad of blue and orange notes. In the toy store, I go down the aisles and buy one of everything, including one giant Hello Kitty doll. I tell the checkout girl we're buying toys for a girls' orphanage with donations.

Aiko kept the car running. I'm just glad to find it's still there. Tiny fits his legs and most of his chest into the trunk. I pile the toys on top of his head, starting with the hard plastic ones. Finally, I lay the gigantic Hello Kitty doll across the back seat. It looks like we bought so many toys they overflowed the trunk. Tiny sneezes, and an electronic rendition of "A Bright Moon" starts.

"Pinch your nose," I yell through the pile of plastic. We're almost at the guard station.

It's the same bored, indifferent guard. Aiko's nerves are only betrayed by the tightness of her smile. I keep my head down, like before.

"I volunteer at a children's hospital," Aiko says. "We picked up some donations from a client."

He waves us through. All three of us let out a breath when we reach the highway. Or, at least, I think Tiny did. One of the toys is singing again.

"Well?" Aiko asks.

I look at her blankly.

"Are you going to call Jones?"

It's a hard pill to swallow, asking Jones for help. I dial Whitney, knowing Jones will answer. Sometimes I hate it when I'm right.

"Afternoon, asshole," Jones says.

I bite back the first greeting that comes to mind. "I'm ready to deal."

A mile passes before he answers. "What do you have?"

"Five years of Hu's financial records, all the forged background checks, and an interview with a high-level enforcer."

Tiny's head surfaces from the pile of toys. A discordant symphony starts in the back seat as he kicks himself free. "Hey! I didn't agree to that."

"What the hell is all that music?" Jones asks. "Who's with you?"

I don't know if Tiny's intentions are genuine, but I bet Jones has ways of finding out. "You want to help April?" I say to Tiny. "We need Jones."

He crosses his arms. When I turn around, I can feel his glare on the back of my head. I wonder if I can keep Tiny in the car against his will.

I hear Jones's deep chuckle on the other end of the line. "No wonder you have no friends."

"It's a good deal," I say.

"Depends on what you want in return."

"The Little Caesar gang kidnapped April. She escaped by killing Hu's son; we have to find her before they do."

"That's it?"

"No. I want protection for my brother's family while they're here. And help getting my brother's family back to the States."

"You haven't asked for anything for yourself."

I don't need Jones to play psychologist. "You interested or not?"

"Fine. I have a place we can meet." He rattles off an address; I hold the phone up to Aiko's ear.

She nods. "I know where that is."

"Send someone to my apartment for my brother and his wife," I tell Jones. "I'll text my brother, tell him to cooperate."

"We have badges," Jones says. "Don't worry about it. You need to take the battery out of your phone when we hang up. Hu has this number."

"You haven't met my brother." We've reached the edge

of Hong Kong. It's almost rush hour. Traffic is tighter; the drivers more aggressive.

"He's a smart-ass like you?"

"You need a bigger vocabulary."

"I'll think of a different word to call you if you don't burn me this time."

"Deal." I think I just made a new friend.

CHAPTER 21

Kevin
Washington, DC, 2023

KEVIN SIPPED HIS yuenyeung while he waited for Saul. The coffee, tea, and milk drink was another reminder of Hong Kong. He should have ordered black coffee. Across the street, he saw his quarry leaving the racquetball gym. A medium-height Asian man, too far away to see his features. It couldn't be. But it had to be. Saul would hopefully settle the question.

"You sent me to take pictures of another man in a locker room." Saul dropped into the chair across from Kevin. "What the hell."

Kevin did enjoy making Saul uncomfortable. "Unavoidable, I'm afraid. I needed to see his torso."

"And you couldn't do your own dirty work?"

"He's trying to frame me; he knows my face." Kevin held out his hand for Saul's phone. "The pictures?"

"I can't believe I'm doing this for you," Saul grumbled as he unlocked his phone.

"You're doing it to keep that promotion you got for the North Korea op," Kevin said. "Let's not pretend."

He flipped through the pictures. The wet torso belonged to a man in his late twenties or early thirties. About the right age. A jagged scar ran from his right kidney around his side almost to his belly button. A wound no one should have survived. Except.

"The tattoo." Kevin recognized the distinctive design from the vases in Hu's private collection. "This design was only made by one artist in Hong Kong. It was sort of a family crest. Hu liked that sort of bullshit."

"You think that man is . . ." Saul shook his head. "It's not possible."

"I leave one fucking loose end." Kevin should have known better. Confirm everything. Especially if the son of the homicidal maniac you used to work with was actually dead. "It's Hu's son." *Fuck, fuck, fuck.*

"You said April opened his abdomen and he lost two liters of blood."

"That's what I pieced together between Dan and April's statements." Kevin zoomed in to see the tattoo more clearly. No, he hadn't made a mistake. The sail of a junk boat with intricate Chinese characters spelling out the family name. *In China, I was in the National People's Congress as a member of the Chinese Communist Party,* Hu had told Kevin. *But I came here as no one, and I built an empire.* A good story if you ignored that his first house in Hong Kong was a mansion. "But I know this tattoo. You can have it translated if you don't believe me."

"You're saying Hu's son has been living a comfortable life in China for nearly ten years under a different name. And he's just decided now, to risk all that to rewrite history and make Hu a good guy."

Kevin kicked himself for not putting the pieces together before. "The Ministry of Public Security. You said he was working there. They manage the Chinese government's censorship regime."

Saul leaned back, considering. "So somehow he survives, gets to China. Then uses his dad's CCP connections to build a new life working in government propaganda."

"Erasing Tiananmen Square is a hell of a lot harder than disappearing a few old records in Hong Kong," Kevin said. "Build a few convincing fakes to replace the records you don't like and it's not so hard to sell a new story." The "official" police reports Kevin had seen on Denton's laptop were clever forgeries.

"The man you asked about, Ryan Sing," Saul said. "He's dead. Like you thought."

Kevin nodded. "Were you able to get details?" He would have pulled the information himself but he knew his intelligence searches were being monitored. Denton would add unauthorized access to Kevin's list of crimes.

"Unfortunately," Saul said. "He was found—"

"Dismembered and stuffed into several vases," Kevin said.

Saul's eyes narrowed. "You're annoying. Did you know that? You interrupt people all the time."

"But I'm right."

"Yeah, it was fucking creepy. I can't unsee it."

"That's how Hu killed someone when he wanted to make a point." Kevin took another sip of his drink and then pushed it away. Creamy, sweet, and bitter all at the same time. He used to love the complicated flavor. He used to thrive in the gray area between upstanding, moral citizens and irredeemable villains. That's why he had agreed to work with Hu in the first place. The agency had told him it was necessary.

"I'll set a meeting with Denton tomorrow," Saul said. "We can settle this now."

Always the bulldozer, Kevin thought. "Denton won't believe you. You said yourself; Hu's son should be dead."

"What exactly are you proposing?" Saul asked. "Do I even want to know?"

"It's not enough to get Denton to back down. We need to neutralize Hu's son."

"Jesus. Kevin. Do you hear yourself? I'm not planning an assassination with you."

"Not planning an assassination with me *again* you mean." Kevin needed to remind Saul what the stakes were. Leverage worked both ways. "Anyway, I didn't say kill. I said neutralize. For the Mackenzies' sake."

"You're doing charity work now," Saul said.

"And people say I'm the asshole," Kevin said. "You might not like my methods but at least I'm thinking about someone other than myself."

Kevin couldn't tell if Saul was feeling shame or indigestion.

"Fine, whatever," Saul said. "We'll do it your way. What do you need?"

"A list of the allies and enemies Hu's son has inside the Chinese Communist Party."

"I'm not going to miss being your errand boy," Saul said.

Kevin stood. "And I won't miss our little heart-to-hearts."

CHAPTER 22

Dan
Hong Kong, 2015

AIKO TAKES US to Aberdeen Harbour. She finds a spot to park the car near the bustling fish market just off the docks.

"This way," she says.

Tiny and I follow her as she weaves through the crowd jostling for space at the booths. A fish market in Hong Kong is an illustrated encyclopedia of marine life. Here, if it swims, it's fair game for dinner. We pass by vats of crabs as big as dinner plates, and then a tank full of a miniature sea monsters trying to crawl up the glass. Aiko steers us toward the bobbing boats at the docks. Fast steps behind us make Tiny and I turn around with alarm.

It's only a fisherman with his gaff hook, chasing an escaping sea cucumber the color of a ripe peach. With their sluglike bodies, it's hard to imagine anyone paying a price worthy of the fisherman's effort, but I know they're considered a delicacy here. Behind the angry fisherman, another man hangs squid to dry on long, horizontal poles mounted on the back of his boat. Their plump, pale white tentacles and triangular mantles sway with the boat, resembling ghosts frozen by the daylight.

"Jones said the blue houseboat, at the end of the dock," Aiko says.

Houseboat is being too kind. The sides are made of rotting plywood. An irregular arrangement of tires protects the sides from bumps and scratches. The tin roof is rusted in large chunks. "Are you sure?" I ask.

Aiko ignores me and steps onto the deck, cluttered with fishing supplies and tangled ropes. Except that these ropes look more decorative than functional. She opens a rickety door. Tiny has to duck his head to enter. We step into a dim room. The inside of the boat doesn't match the outside at all. The walls are sturdy and plumb. Maybe even reinforced. A man and a woman, each with a gun at their hip, sit at a small table. They must be the agents that picked up William and Marge at the house.

"Nice of you to show up." It's William's voice, from behind me.

I pull myself up to full height and feel the weight of my gut on my spine, then turn to face him.

"What the hell is going on?" William demands. "Who is this goon? Why didn't the picture arrive?"

"Goon?" Tiny looks offended.

I step between Tiny and William. "You kidnapped his daughter," I tell Tiny in Cantonese. "He's a little upset."

"Could we speak English?" Marge says from her spot on the bench. She has her knitting in her lap. Even my untrained eye can see the mistakes in the pattern. "And could someone *please* tell us what's going on?"

"April escaped." I decide to leave out the detail of the blood on the carpet. "This is Tiny Clint. He says he'll help us find her."

"Tiny?" my brother asks, fists forming. "The one who kidnapped her?" I forgot that I mentioned Tiny's name in front of William. Luckily, I'm already standing between them. It takes both Marge and me to hold him back.

"Would you stop?" I snap. "I didn't have time to get into the whole story. If you'd calm down for one minute, maybe we can figure things out."

Reluctantly, William takes a seat on the bench next to Marge. I pull Tiny to the other side of the room next to the agents.

Everyone's looking at me like I know what to do next. I straighten myself again and try to look confident. "First things first," I say to Tiny. "Why are you willing to help us find April when you kidnapped her? And speak English. So everyone can understand you."

Tiny has the grace to look ashamed. There are even tears in his eyes. "That was before I knew."

"Before you knew what?" I ask through gritted teeth.

Tiny looks at me like I should know the answer. "That she was the love of my life."

That's a twist. "You're in love with April."

He uncrosses his arms, leans forward. The agents near him inch closer, just in case. "You should have seen her fight when we took her. She . . ." He searches for words.

William's face is turning red.

It might be better if William doesn't understand Tiny. "Use Cantonese if you need to," I say. "I'll translate."

Tiny looks grateful. "She was as fierce as a tiger, as graceful as a swan. It took three of us to take her alive."

Red clouds my vision. The male agent near Tiny shoots me a warning look. I realize my fists are clenched and I've taken a step toward Tiny. William's not the only one with anger management issues.

"I stayed with her every minute, to make sure no one hurt her. To make sure we returned her safely. I'm not the only one who noticed she was beautiful. But they sent me away on . . ." He glances at the agents. "Other business. Just for a couple hours."

This time I'm aware of my speeding pulse, even as I connect the dots. April killed Hu's son. Tiny armed her with a knife. She wouldn't kill unless she had to. She only escaped, and killed, when she was left alone, without Tiny's protection.

I answer in Cantonese, to keep William from overhearing. "You left her with Hu's son, knowing he would try to rape her."

"What did you say?" my brother demands.

I ignore him.

Tiny holds up his hands. His words stumble over each other. "They lied to me. They said Hu's son was gone on business for the day. But I gave her a knife, just in case. And I told her how to get out of the neighborhood and a place where she could hide. I promised I would come find her if something happened."

I switch back to English. "How do they know you helped her escape?"

"She dropped the knife while she was running. My men recognized it." He steps closer to me with a sincere plea in his eyes. "I must prove my love to her. That she can trust me. Now your friend is safe, her parents are safe. We must go find her."

"I'm not sure I trust you either."

Tiny aims his pleads at Marge and William, across the room. "I am very sorry," he says in English. "To have hurt your daughter. Please believe me. I love her. She is beautiful and smart and I am . . ." He rubs his hands together and stares at them while he searches for words. "I am unworthy. I must save her. I will do anything."

I look at William, preparing to intervene when his temper inevitably flares. But William doesn't look angry. "Makes perfect sense to me."

Tiny grins, the happiest I've ever seen him. "I knew you would understand."

"I *understand*, that doesn't mean I approve." William's jaw tightens as his eyes narrow. "You touch my daughter again and I'll—"

"Let's just concentrate on finding April," I say. William shouldn't be making threats he can't follow through on; Tiny could crack his spine without breaking a sweat.

Thankfully, the door opens and Jones enters with Whitney close behind. Whitney goes straight to Aiko, folding her into a hug that says they're more than friends. I nearly got Whitney's girlfriend killed.

Jones looks at the lovesick Tiny. "Ryan Sing. A good catch."

I forget that Tiny has a real name sometimes.

"Are you the one in charge?" my brother asks Jones.

Annoyance flickers across Jones's face. "Yes, Agent Jones, CIA." He holds out his hand with a superficial smile.

William accepts the handshake, then turns to Whitney. "And you're his partner?"

Figures William would treat this like a goddamn business meeting. It's all he knows.

Jones sighs. Then, in a blink, he puts on the official distant-but-friendly demeanor used by service providers the world over. "Mr. and Mrs. Mackenzie, I understand how confusing this all must be for you, and I'm sorry for that. However, in the interests of your daughter's safety, I'd like to save the explanations for later. We have a safe house prepared for you. The officers who picked you up at Dan's apartment will take you there."

William shakes his head. "I'm not going. My daughter needs me, and I'm going to help. Just tell me what I can do."

"I appreciate your feelings, but in this situation the best thing you can do is go to the safe house so we can concentrate on finding your daughter."

William doesn't like hearing that explanation from Jones any more than he liked hearing it from me. He pulls himself up to his full height, barely contained anger stiffening his shoulders.

"I might not be a professional whatever you are, but I can hold my own."

I step out of William's line of sight and send a pleading look to Marge.

"Honey, I think we should listen to him," Marge says.

I recognize the shame clouding William's eyes. She's only

reminded him of how little he can help. "Don't tell me what to do," he yells.

Marge absorbs the vicious look without blinking, somehow understanding his pain through her own.

Jones rolls his eyes. "Would you tell him?" he asks me in Cantonese.

"He won't listen to Dan," Tiny answers for me. "April told me they've been estranged for years."

"You think you're such a big man?" Jones asks William, switching back to English. "Fine." Jones pulls a knife from his pocket. With a flick of his wrist, the blade snaps into place. He holds it out to William with the blade pointed toward himself. "Try to cut me."

My brother stares at the knife. "You can't be serious."

Aiko looks between them. "This is a terrible idea."

"William, I know we've had our issues," I say. "But please believe me. You should go to the safe house."

It's not in William to leave a challenge unanswered. He takes the knife from Jones, weighs it in his palm, then grips it tightly. I've fought men like Jones. Without training, my brother has no chance. He'll be humiliated, emasculated. There's nothing I can do.

William launches himself at Jones with his arm fully extended, the knife held straight out. A beginner's mistake. Extending your arm restricts your freedom of movement, and it leaves the elbow joint vulnerable to attack. Jones sweeps away the arm, slams a forearm against William's elbow. With a sharp cry, William loses the knife. The boat rocks.

William stumbles and Jones throws him to the carpet,

then retrieves the knife William so confidently held seconds earlier.

A quiver in his jaw betrays William's disappointment. His face's ruddy hue could be mistaken for anger, except for the downturned mouth and glistening eyes.

"That's enough, Jones." It's hard not to attack him myself. "Put your toy away."

Another flick of Jones's wrist hides the blade. "This isn't your game," he tells William. "You want to do something for your daughter? Stay alive so you can take her home."

I step between Jones and William. "I said that's enough." Surprisingly, William accepts the hand I offer to help him up. I hold the grip for a beat longer than necessary. "I'll let you know the second I have something."

He nods. I think he's afraid of how his voice will sound if he speaks. Marge huddles next to him. Their CIA escorts give Jones a look before taking the unhappy couple off the boat.

"They don't let you out very often, do they?" I ask Jones. "You could have handled that better."

He slips the knife back in this pocket. A hint of regret flashes across his face. "No, I don't think so. Now he'll listen. We don't have time to waste on being nice."

"Still," Aiko says.

Jones ignores her. "Whitney, you and Aiko can use the delta safe house. Stay there until you hear from me."

Then it's only me, the cranky CIA agent, and the lovesick gangster.

Jones takes a seat at the table and motions for me to follow suit. "We stopped by your apartment and let ourselves in." He pulls my laptop and a sheaf of papers out of his bag. I recognize the envelopes with the photos of April.

"You want the files on the Little Caesar gang before we start looking for April," I say.

He looks at me for a long second. "You really think I'm that much of an asshole, don't you?"

I shrug.

"Hu's focus now is on finding April. That's a problem for us, because he has more people than I do."

I wait for him to finish the thought.

"I'd like to send a couple agents to stage an attack on one of his valuable assets. With your knowledge, I think we can pick a good target."

I may have underestimated him. It's a good plan.

"Now, Mr. Sing—"

"I prefer Clint," Tiny says.

"Fine. Clint, then." Jones brings out a blank page, but leaves his pen on the table. "I need to know why you're helping us."

Tiny puffs out his chest. "Because I love April."

The agent's mouth drops open a millimeter. He looks at me for confirmation.

"He seems to be telling the truth."

Jones pulls out the first photo of April. The image of her bruised face makes me wince again. "Did you fall in love with her before or after you beat her up?"

"I didn't—" Tiny brushes his fingers over her face. "She fought hard. I had to subdue her to keep the boys from using their knives or guns."

Those hawk eyes of Jones focus on Tiny for a long minute,

the photo forgotten. I shove it back in the envelope; it's too painful to see. Finally, Jones relents. "Just when I think I've seen everything."

While I search my laptop for good break-in targets, Jones meticulously interviews Tiny. When exactly did April escape? Three hours ago. What did Tiny tell April? The name of a friend who would get her out of Jardine's Lookout, and an address to meet her. How does Tiny know that April used the contact he gave her? Because the contact called Tiny. So he's sure April is no longer in Jardine's Lookout? Yes. What's the address where April was dropped off at? Where's the address where Tiny said he would meet her? And she hasn't arrived at the meetup location? No. How is he sure? Someone would have called.

Then Jones turns his questions to me.

"Where did April do her studying?"

I should know this. I stare at the keys on my laptop. "I don't know."

"What about the names of her friends? Roommates? Was she dating anyone?"

In all our conversations, I never asked. I try to remember what we did talk about. Me. My drinking. How her dad was. My drinking. Occasionally, she complained about her roommates.

"She wasn't close to her roommates."

Jones waits expectantly for the answers to the other questions.

The list of places I've jotted down on the folder next to my laptop seems inadequate. "Look, I don't know about a boyfriend. Or who she hung out with. We didn't talk about that sort of stuff."

"You could have told me that before I sent her parents away," Jones says. Before I can answer, he takes out his phone to make a call. "Interview the parents," he says to whomever answers. "Find out if she has any friends or contacts here she might ask for help."

Tiny shakes his head disapprovingly at me. "She was only trying to help you, and you dragged her into this."

Jones raises his eyebrows as he puts the phone down. "An enforcer with a heart of gold. Who knew." Then, to me, "Do you know where April hung out on her downtime? Places on campus she liked?"

I don't know. I open my mouth to answer, but the repetition sticks in my throat.

Jones sighs. "Let me guess. You don't know."

I should have been supporting her instead of the other way around.

"We'll have to start with where she was dropped off then."

I know the Sheung Wan neighborhood by reputation. There are a lot of traditional medicine shops there. My roommate is always trying to tell me about some special miracle cure he picked up there made from dried seahorses or gecko testicles. Aside from some questionable medical cures, the area is fairly safe. It's mostly populated by locals who were pushed out of the central district by high real estate prices.

Jones takes my laptop without asking and pulls up a map. He points to the intersection where April was dropped off, near the International Finance Centre mall. It's only a mile from the University of Hong Kong.

"That's her college. She'd probably try to get to campus," I say.

"That's my guess too," Jones says.

Two cell phones ring at once, Jones's and Tiny's.

"You left your cell phone on?" Jones says. "The one Hu gave you? You idiot. He keeps tracking software on all those phones." Tiny's about to defend himself, but Jones already has his own phone up to his ear. "I have to take this. Turn your goddamn phone off and take the battery out."

Tiny answers it instead. His face breaks into a wide grin. "That's good news, my old friend. You have my thanks. We will be there as soon as we can. Don't open the door for anyone but me."

"You should have called me ten minutes ago," Jones says into his phone. "I said call me immediately if—"

Tiny taps Jones on the shoulder.

"What?" the agent snaps.

"That was my burn phone. I know where she is."

Jones's surprised expression only lasts a second, then he returns to berating whomever is on the phone. "Immediately means the second you know, asshole. If you hear anything else, call me *immediately*."

"She finally made her way to our meeting spot," Tiny says.

"She won't be safe there for long," Jones says. "That was my signals guy. Someone spotted April, and Hu has moved people into the neighborhood to find her. She already had a run-in with one of them, left him with a broken nose."

Tiny pushes away from the table. "Then let's go."

"Calm down, cowboy. You get to go to a nice hotel room

with a friend of mine. You can write April a love ballad or something."

"I have to go with you," Tiny says.

Because Tiny told his friend not to open the door for anyone else. "Just call your friend back and introduce me," I say. "Give him a code word so he'll know to open the door."

"It's not a *gweilo* neighborhood. Two white men will stick out like a sore thumb."

"And after Hu's men recognize you, you'll lead them right to April," Jones says.

"Just give me a disguise."

Jones snorts. "A disguise? Sure. I have some magic pants that will make you a foot shorter."

Tiny, adamant, crosses his arms. "I'm going with you."

I speak before Jones can piss him off more. "I'll tell April how you helped us. She'll know everything."

"You don't understand." Tiny scowls. "It's not just about April. My friend has taken a big risk for me. The neighbors will notice you and start talking. My friend could get hurt."

Jones narrows his eyes. "If there's no way for us to get in without attracting attention, how did a white girl with red hair get in?"

"There's a nail salon in the same building," Tiny says. "But no one will believe you're there for a pedicure." He uncrosses his arms and steps around Jones. "I'm going to get April. You two can wait for me here."

Jones intercepts Tiny with one broad palm to his chest. A muscle in Tiny's jaw twitches. It's hard to guess who would win. Tiny has the advantage of height, weight, and strength. But Jones is wily. Both know how to fight from the gutter.

"Even assuming I buy your love story, you need to lose this knight-in-shining-armor fantasy. Hu has fifteen men closing in on April's last known location. Are you going to fight them by yourself?"

Tiny dwarfs Jones by a good foot. "I will if I have to."

No matter how this fight goes, one of my allies is going to get hurt. I need both of them in good condition. I push myself between them until the bulk around my midsection forces them apart. "What door does the salon use to get deliveries?"

"What the hell does that matter?" asks Jones.

Tiny ignores Jones, thinking. "There's a freight entrance in the back of the building. All the businesses on the first floor share it."

Despite himself, Jones follows my plan. "And from that freight entrance you can get into the hallway where the apartments are?"

I take advantage of their calm to push them further apart with my hands. "How about we make a delivery, in a very large cardboard box, to one of those businesses? Dress Tiny up in a service uniform, add a hat, and he'll be nearly invisible. I'll ride in the box while you keep the van running. Best case April rides out in the box with me. Worst case, the three of us fight our way out."

"You're smarter than you look," Jones says reluctantly.

"Thanks. When can we leave?"

CHAPTER 23

Dan
Hong Kong, 2015

THAT's HOW I end up in the cargo area of a van, sweating inside a cardboard box labeled Styling Chair in Chinese. Jones found some green uniforms in a closet on the boat. The rough fabric scratches at my armpits, where even I can feel the circles of sweat. In the front of the van, Jones and Tiny argue like an old married couple. In my ear. All three of us are wearing earpieces. I spend the long ride hoping they don't start punching each other before we get there. Finally, the sound of the highway fades.

The roar of engines is replaced by honking horns and the sputtering staccato bursts of scooters maneuvering through slow traffic. When the van stops, I hear the scattered conversations of a busy sidewalk bleed through the thin metal wall.

"Well?" Jones snaps at Tiny, in my earpiece. "Go already."

"I'm going," Tiny says. But it's a long second before I hear the door open. Tiny's nervous. I've never known him to be nervous before. The back doors on the van creak open; the sounds of the street get louder. A groan from the suspension system means Tiny's jumped into the cargo area. I hear the clunk of metal and the ramp for the dolly extending out. The foot of the dolly squirms underneath my box, and I'm thrown against the frame as Tiny tilts me back.

I bite my lip, hard, to keep from swearing. "Live cargo," I whisper from my cardboard cage. "Would you be careful?"

"Oh, sorry," Tiny says.

"No talking to the box," Jones says.

I'm wheeled down the ramp. To his credit, Tiny eases the box onto the street. There's nothing he can do about the uneven sidewalk, though. I brace my shoulder against the dolly and absorb my bruises silently.

"Coast is clear so far," Jones says. "But my signals man says Hu's men are close."

Tiny pounds his fist on a door; I can hear it rattle in its hinges. "Delivery for the salon," he says, when it opens.

"Down the hall and to the right," answers a voice. "I'll prop open the double doors for you."

I feel the dolly get pushed up a slight ledge, and we're in the building. Smells just about like my apartment building. Two minutes later I'm pushed into an elevator that definitely smells like my apartment building. After the ding, and a breath of fresh air, Tiny pushes the dolly into a hallway. When he stops, I hear a light knock on a wooden door.

"It's me," Tiny says softly.

I wait for the door to open, for the dolly to get wheeled in, but nothing happens.

"Leung," Tiny says. "It's me."

"What's wrong?" Jones says.

"I don't know. He's not answering."

"Then how about you let yourself in. You have five minutes, tops."

The doorknob rattles, then turns. "The door's not locked," Tiny says.

That's all I need to hear. I take my knife and cut out an exit. The mutilated box will be all the evidence Hu's men need, but maybe they've been here already.

I push past Tiny's pale face and into Leung's apartment. The small living room/kitchen area is empty. Tiny breaks free from his paralysis and follows. I find a bathroom—empty. I push open the bedroom door and see a man's legs sticking out from underneath the bed. There are signs of a fight: books pushed off a nightstand, a plant knocked over.

Oh God, oh God, oh God.

I run to the other side of the room, around the bed. He's on his stomach, still breathing. I feel for a pulse to be sure. He stirs when I turn him over. There's only one bruise on his face, nothing bleeding. Hu's men are normally more thorough than that, but maybe they were in a hurry.

Tiny squeezes in by me. "Leung! What happened? Where's April?"

Leung's eyes blink open. He sits up, looks around, momentarily confused. "Ryan, you came. I told her to wait."

"Who took her?" Tiny demands. "Tell me anything you can remember."

He shakes his head. "No one. She left. I told her to wait. I tried to make her wait."

For the second time today, I feel a vise around my heart release. "Hu's men haven't been here."

Leung shrinks back from me. "Who are you?"

"A friend," Tiny assures him. "What happened to April? Where did she go?"

Leung leans against the bed, his head in his hands. "She said they were close behind her. That they would find her here and I would get hurt. All she wanted was a little money for a cab before she moved on."

Poor, good-hearted April.

"Are you Dan?" Leung asks me.

I nod.

"She said you would come. She said to meet her where and when you were happy once. She said you would know what that meant."

Where I was happy once. The memory startles me with its clarity. The San Francisco Zoo. It was one of the rare trips Carol and I took with my brother and Marge. April wasn't more than eight. It was obvious that things between Carol and I were rough. Our flight the day before had been delayed several hours, and everyone was tired from the jet lag. But April was so excited about the giant panda exhibit at the San Francisco Zoo, she pestered everyone until we hauled ourselves out of bed. After a night short of sleep, and a full day at the zoo, everyone was ready to go but April. There was a feeding scheduled at four o'clock, and she begged us to stay. I promised April we could, and Carol's fragile mood snapped. We argued. April was in tears over the possibility of a broken promise. Finally, Marge dragged Will and Carol away for some overpriced coffee, muttering under her breath.

April and I were left alone to wait for the momentous panda feeding. For all the trouble I caused, the feeding consisted of a zookeeper pushing in a giant pile of bamboo which the pandas lazily consumed. April didn't look disappointed, though. She watched the pandas chew on their bamboo leaves with bright eyes, then turned back to me, trouble creasing her soft face.

"Are you happy, Uncle Dan?"

I had to think about it. Both my brother and my wife were pissed at me. That week I had lied for Mack, providing an alibi for one of the many nights he spent at a hotel instead of at home. But staring into April's hopeful green eyes, with her red hair still disheveled from sleeping in the car on the way to the zoo, the only thing I could say was "yes." I was happy because I had made April happy. It was as simple as that.

Hong Kong is not San Francisco, of course. But there is a giant panda exhibit at Ocean Park. I check my watch. Ocean Park closed an hour ago; she must mean tomorrow.

"Dan?" Jones interrupts my thoughts. "You know what April meant?"

I nod, then remember Jones can't hear gestures. "Yeah."

"Then maybe you two would like to get the fuck out of there."

It's hard to argue with that.

Tiny thanks Leung quickly. I climb back into my cardboard prison, then hang on for the bumpy ride toward the van. Once the doors close me in and the engine rumbles, I abandon the box and sit on the hard metal floor second-guessing myself. Would April really remember that day at the zoo as well as I do? I think so, because of what happened later.

Two weeks after the ill-fated trip to San Francisco, I arrived at William's house for dinner alone. Over mashed potatoes, I announced that Carol and I were divorcing. April ran, crying, into her bedroom. After a second of surprise, I followed. I didn't expect April would care much one way or the other. She and Carol had never been close. I found April face down on her pillow screaming in the way only children know how. She was repeating something over and over; I had to listen hard to understand.

"My fault, my fault, my fault," she said against the wet pillow.

I promised myself it would be the last time I failed her.

"April, sweetie," I said.

Her litany paused.

"Why would you think it's your fault?"

William watched carefully at the door, ready to find me guilty of another crime.

"At the zoo," she managed. "By the pandas. She wanted to go and I wanted to stay and you said we should stay. It was my fault you argued."

If she hadn't been so serious, I would have laughed. I swallowed over the lump in my throat. "Our divorce has nothing to do with that."

April sniffed back her tears, a little calmer. "What happened?"

How could I paraphrase four tumultuous years? The tangled knot of betrayals, disappointments, and failures that overwhelmed us? At the time, I thought the blame was half mine, half Carol's. Now I know it was more like a 75-25 split. I cheated on her. I drank too much. But before all that, she was the one who shut me out. She married a cocky, strong police cadet. Neither of us expected her to end up with an alcoholic, depressed almost-detective.

"It's hard to explain," I told April. "But it wasn't anything to do with you."

April buried her head in my shoulder; William nodded his approval. I think it was the last time he approved of anything I did.

"Would you mind sharing?" Jones says in my ear.

I blink my eyes open to my jarring reality, a hard floor and a stuffy cargo area and my kidnapped niece. "Sharing?"

"The meet, asshole. Where are we picking up April?"

"The giant panda exhibit at Ocean Park. 16:00 tomorrow."

"Tomorrow?" Tiny says. "We can't leave her alone tonight."

Tiny's insistence jogs another memory loose, something more recent. About a class she was taking outside of her major, just for fun. She told me about it over dinner.

"Hang on, let me think," I say.

That was a particularly bad night for me. I always drank more on the anniversary of Mack's death. Think past Mack's ghost, I tell myself. April's course. It was a . . . zoology course. Part of it was held at Ocean Park, interacting up close with the animals. She made friends with the one of the zookeepers on the penguin exhibit; the zookeeper offered to let her witness the much-anticipated birth of Ocean Park's new king penguin. If her semester had lasted just a couple weeks longer, she would have.

She chose to meet at the zoo because that's where she plans to spend the night. Ocean Park is a brilliant place to hide. It's a common destination for tourists. The government takes crime there very seriously. Even Hu's men will be reluctant to cause any collateral damage. It's a sprawling complex with lots of nooks and crannies. And her friend will be able to get her in after hours.

"I know where April is," I say.

"Took you long enough," Jones says.

CHAPTER 24

Dan
Hong Kong, 2015

JONES DRIVES ANOTHER ten minutes, then stops the van. Through the small, grimy window in the back I can see a parking lot behind a convenience store. I hear Jones open the door over my earpiece, then slam it shut so loud, I wince. "Everyone out," he barks. "We're switching cars."

Tiny and I follow Jones to a blue sedan parked a few spaces away. I let Tiny have the front seat so he can enjoy the pleasure of Jones's company. Jones has been on the phone almost constantly since I told him April was at the zoo. He's not just rude to me—it's everyone.

His phone rings again as he starts the sedan. "The team is in place at the warehouse?" he asks.

He means Hu's pottery warehouse, where Hu fills counterfeit antique vases with powder cocaine. His buyers pay for the drugs inside the vases, but on paper the money looks like it went for ornately decorated pieces of ancient pottery.

In most cases, if the authorities even catch on, the drugs are gone by the time the shipment is tracked. The buyers pretend outrage at having paid so much for a forgery. Jones pulls the sedan into traffic smoothly, despite the phone pressed to his ear. It's officially rush hour now. Congested Hong Kong roads are not for the faint of heart.

"Tell them to shoot the place up enough to break a few windows," Jones says. "And use the M82 to destroy the engine blocks in all the trucks."

Here, like anywhere, crime syndicates are always jockeying for position. When the pottery warehouse gets attacked, Hu will assume it's one of his business rivals. He can't leave the insult unanswered, or his competitors will smell blood in the water.

"Did you get the names of those zookeepers for me? Hang on." He hits a button and I hear the hiss of the speaker. "Now list the names."

A female voice, not Whitney or Aiko, lists off five names.

"Any of them familiar?" Jones asks me.

The shame I felt in the back of the van returns. I can't even remember the name of April's friend. "No."

Jones shakes his head at my ignorance. "I think that's all we need—"

"The course catalog," I say. It's not quite redemption, but I'm not useless.

"The course catalog what?" Jones snaps.

"It listed the zookeeper as one of the instructors. The course catalogs are all online now. You can look it up."

"No need," says the female voice. "I have her enrollment records right here."

Of course they do. Keys click in the background.

"Here it is," she says. "Mei Han Shih."

"Send me that number. And call once the team at the warehouse is done so I know when we can move on the zoo." Jones ends the call.

The thought of Hu's precious pottery under attack makes me smile a little. He moves thousands of dollars of drugs through that warehouse. I just wish I could be there to help.

Jones hands his phone to me. "Dial the number in that text message. It's Mei Han's office."

The prospect of hearing April's voice makes my heart skip. The phone rings until it goes to Mei's voicemail. "You've reached Mei Han, Avian Veterinary Resident at Ocean Park. Please leave a message." Then a slight pause. "All media inquiries should be directed to the Ocean Park Public Relations office." She must be getting calls from reporters about the baby king penguin. The consciousness of Hong Kong shrugs over people living in stacked cages due to high real estate prices, but swoons over the birth of a cute, fuzzy animal.

No, I don't want to leave a message. Maybe if I make a pest of myself, she'll answer. The fourth time I call she picks up.

"If you're a reporter—" she says.

"I'm April's uncle."

There's a long pause. "April?" She hasn't hung up yet, but she's close. April would have told her to be cautious.

"I get it. You don't want to admit she's there." I have to give Mei Han a way she can trust me. "I'll call back and leave a message. Have April listen to it. She'll know my voice."

The phone clicks. I'm not sure if she's waiting for my voicemail or if she's decided I'm not worth her time.

I call back and wait impatiently for the beep that signals I can talk. For one terrifying second, my throat closes. I don't know what to say to April. "It's me." The cheap upholstery squeaks as I shift. "I have help. We can pick you up tonight. Your parents are safe."

"Give her my number," Jones says.

I look at him blankly.

"My phone number, idiot."

Of course. "We can't use my phone anymore, you can reach me at this number." I read back the number twice and hang up. We're at a standstill in traffic. A light rain has started. The reflection of the stoplights in the windshield stain the water red. Every second on my watch passes like ten. *Please, just let her be safe.* There's a lot I deserve for everything I've done. But that's me, not April. She shouldn't have to pay my debts. The phone comes to life in my clenched hand.

I hold it to my ear as I let out a breath. "April?"

"Uncle," she says. "You remembered."

I squeeze my eyes shut, feeling Tiny and Jones watching. "I'm so sorry." I need to say it again; I need to keep saying it for the rest of my life.

"You're sorry for being early?" It's good to hear her smile.

"How are you?" What a ridiculous question. "I mean, are you injured?"

"A few bruises, that's all. When can you get here?"

I look at Jones. He can only spare me one annoyed glance. Traffic is moving again. "Why don't you put her on speaker so we can hear what she's saying?"

Of course.

"Who's we?" April asks.

"I'm here!" Tiny looks besotted again. "I'm so glad you made it. We were worried."

"Ryan." April knows Tiny's real name? Exactly how much did they talk during the last two days? Her tone isn't warm, but it isn't angry either.

A cascade of honking starts as Jones cuts off another driver. "Are we done with the reunions?"

"That'd be Jones," I say, for April's benefit.

"Tom Jones, CIA," he finishes for me. "I'm helping your uncle out in return for a favor."

"The CIA?" April sounds bewildered. "You know someone at the CIA?"

Explaining would mean going into her father's business troubles. "It's a long story."

"Can you put Mei on the phone?" Jones asks.

"I'm here," Mei says.

"The official map only shows one entrance to the park. It's a bit too exposed for my taste. Are there any other entrances?"

"There's the old Tai Shue Wan entrance, on Shum Wan. We only open it for Chinese New Year, but I could ask the night guard—"

"We shouldn't involve anyone else," Jones says. "There must be a gate you close on Shum Wan road to keep people from using that entrance. Where's that?"

There's a pause while she thinks. "About a mile before the entrance."

"Can you have April out there in an hour? Without driving?"

"Sure."

"But—" Tiny starts to protest.

"One hour," Jones says. "At the gate to the old entrance. Got it, Mei? April?"

"One hour," Mei and April say together. Jones hangs up without letting me say goodbye.

Tiny has his fists clenched, ready to start swinging. "One hour is too long. Call them back."

Jones shakes his head. "We need Hu distracted, remember? That means we have to wait until he responds to the attack on his warehouse." If he's worried about Tiny, it doesn't show. He dials another number. "Tell the parents we found their daughter and she's safe. We should be at the safe house with April in two hours . . . I need you to arrange transport out of the country for the family . . . No, keep the safe house ready for Ryan. We'll need it soon." He hangs up without saying what his plans for me are.

CHAPTER 25

Kevin
Washington, DC, 2023

A GILDED BED frame. Royal blue curtains. A premier view of the Capitol. *This room will set the scene perfectly.* And the ridiculously large closet meant Kevin would have enough room for his surprise guests.

"Our hotel provides everything you need to make your conference attendees comfortable." The concierge held up a faux leather-bound menu. "There is a chef available 24/7 who will make anything you like to order."

Kevin noticed the concierge's starched blue uniform was the same royal blue as the curtains. "Everything looks good. But, if you wouldn't mind, my co-chair and I would like to confer. Could we meet you at the concierge desk in ten minutes?"

"Of course, sir." The concierge bowed slightly.

Saul gestured at the opulent granite counter in the

bathroom. "One night in this hotel room is one week of my pay. Are you sure we need this?"

"Half a week," Kevin corrected. "We're splitting the cost, remember?"

"You didn't answer my question," Saul said. "Why do we need to use the fanciest hotel in DC?"

"When I invite Hu's son to meet me here, he will interpret is as a sign of respect," Kevin said. "He'll expect me to bribe him or beg for mercy."

"He might be smarter than his father," Saul said.

Kevin laughed. "I doubt it. He's a wannabe strongman without any henchmen. He'll offer me a job as an informant in return for throwing Denton off my trail."

"You think you always know what people are going to do," Saul said. "But you've been wrong before."

The remark stung; Kevin kept his face neutral. "I'm right most of the time." *Just not all the time.*

"How comforting."

Kevin was imagining the op in his head, playing things out to find any flaws in his plan. Leave the closet door ajar a tiny bit. Angle Denton's chair so he can see through the opening. There was room enough for a second chair, if their second guest wanted one. Kevin's plan would work. Probably.

Kevin straightened to his full height and allowed his anger to sharpen his expression. Saul stepped back slightly, enough that Kevin knew he had intimidated him.

"You want a job without risk?" Kevin asked. "Be a fucking accountant."

"Hu's son might kill us," Saul said.

"You don't have to be here," Kevin reminded him. "Only me."

Saul frowned. "But I—"

"Don't trust me, I know." Kevin said. "I guess you'll have to choose: hide out in this hotel room to make sure I'm doing what I said I'd do, or do your part then walk away."

"You're not worried at all," Saul said, "Even about yourself?"

Kevin had imagined how he might die in this room. By a gunshot maybe, falling against the Salvador Dalí-inspired carpet. Or, more likely, stabbed and bleeding out against the pristine white duvet covering the king size bed. Stabbing was more likely. Hu's son preferred the same weapon his father had.

"You still don't get it," Kevin said. "What our job is."

"You're going to lecture me?" Saul scoffed. "We wouldn't be in this mess if you had done your job eight years ago. All you had to do was—"

"Our job is to shield and protect," Kevin said. "The company says jump and you ask how high. But do you ever ask who you're helping? Who you're hurting?"

"Those are dangerous questions," Saul said.

"Tomorrow, Hu's son will either kill me or be sent home by the CCP. Either way, he stops spreading lies and he will no longer be a threat to the Mackenzies. *That* is our job."

"Is that what you think of yourself? That you're a fucking saint?" Saul nearly knocked a lamp over as he swept his arm in a semicircle around the room. "I can't die here. I have a wife and a daughter. It's easier to sacrifice yourself when no one will miss you."

Asshole. Kevin wouldn't rise to the bait. "Just make sure you bring our guest tomorrow. I'll take care of everything else."

Outside, Kevin told himself it was the summer humidity making him sweat. Irving, his little brother in the Big Brother program, would miss him. Jackson, his longtime friend, would miss him. Navy might miss him. A short list, to be sure. But maybe that was the point.

Kevin had kept the list short deliberately. He knew his job. And Saul was right about one thing: emotional attachments were a liability.

CHAPTER 26

Dan
Hong Kong, 2015

JONES DRIVES THE car to a small parking lot behind a restaurant. Clouds of steam and the sizzle of deep fryers waft out a service door, propped open with someone's shoe. My appetite sharpens, then wanes as the smell of the dumpster seeps in, pungent with expired seafood. Jones taps his fingers on the steering wheel impatiently. Aside from our headlights, the parking lot is dark. The shadows cast by the buildings around us leave plenty of places to hide.

I'm impatient to get to April. "Can I ask what we're—"

"Supplies," Jones says.

A man in an apron emerges from the service door carrying two cardboard boxes. They're about the size DVD players might come in. Jones pops the trunk; the man loads the packages without saying a word.

Twenty minutes after we leave with our supplies and

fifty minutes after we talked to April, we turn on to Shum Wan Road. On our right, a marina glitters with lights and bobbing boats. We pass the rock wall that protects the marina. Jones kills the headlights. The ocean, gray and dark, lurks on the right side of the road. Dense vegetation looms on the left. A good place to dump bodies. Ahead, a puddle on the road reflects a wan crescent moon. I can just see a small booth in the center of two gates blocking the road.

"Shit-shit-shit," Jones says softly. He stops well short of the gate, then reverses around the curve until we can't see the booth.

It's the first time I've seen Jones look scared. I think of William and Marge, patiently waiting for their daughter to arrive, thinking she's safe. "What did you see?"

Jones points. "Car tracks beyond the puddle. We're not the only ones here." Jones wraps a white-knuckled hand around the steering wheel. "Hu's men must have tracked April here somehow."

I stare into the dark forest that both hides and traps April. "You two can stay in the car if you want. I'm going after her."

"I'm going too!" Tiny sounds offended.

"Wait one damn minute," Jones snaps. "Let me think. They must have tracked April's cab to the zoo. Hu doesn't have the connections to listen in on my sat phone. They're here because this is a better place to break in. They don't know we're meeting here; they just think April is on the grounds somewhere."

Tiny's hand is resting on the door handle. "So let's find April before they do."

Jones's phone vibrates in his hand; he frowns. "It's a text message from Hu to your number. I had all of them forwarded to my phone."

I grab the phone from him. I say April's name under my breath, the way Marge did. As if wishing hard enough will bring her home safe.

First we find April and throw her in with the tigers, then we're coming for you.

Think like a cop, I tell myself. Panicking won't save her. "Hu's taunting me. He wants to lure me to the zoo. That means he doesn't know we're here."

"I wish we could warn her," Tiny whispers.

Jones gets out, then waits expectantly for us to follow. A button on the remote pops the trunk open with a soft click. He pulls the flaps back on one of the boxes to reveal a collection of gear. We called them active shooter kits when I was on the force. The bulletproof vests are government issue, but the guns aren't. The serial numbers have been filed off.

"You two get to share a box," Jones says softly. "I wasn't planning on the third wheel." He puts on the vest, straps a holster around his waist, and sheaths a knife around his leg. A small vest pocket holds a plastic cylinder six inches long. Jones taps it with one gloved finger. "Glow stick. In case you need a silent signal." He looks at us both sternly. "Follow my lead. Think guerrilla tactics, not heroics. My intel says Hu has somewhere between five and ten men on the search for April. We're outnumbered."

I don't need lectures from Jones. I open the box of

supplies that Tiny and I will be sharing. It's obvious Tiny won't fit in the bulletproof vest or the gloves. I take those. He takes the automatic rifle. I take the pistol. We play tug-of-war over the night vision goggles for a few seconds, until I point out his weapon doesn't require as much aim. I have twenty shots including the spare magazine. I don't like that math.

Tiny weighs the automatic rifle in his hand. "These are Hu's weapons. I recognize them."

Jones nods. "We stole them when we hit the warehouse. Will save us some awkward questions later, assuming we all walk out."

Assuming.

We walk the last quarter mile to the gate, hugging the cover of the forest. When we reach the two cars sitting on the road, the ones that left the tire tracks, I know our caution has only wasted time. The engine is barely warm. Hu's men were in the forest before we started walking.

I curse my panting breaths as we climb over the gate. Tiny and Jones leap over with practiced grace, politely ignoring my labors. I'm not in any shape for this.

After a few steps, the jungle closes in behind us. Even the lapping sounds of the ocean are gone, overwhelmed by the chattering and singing of the creatures around us. We pause to let Tiny's eyes adjust to the new level of darkness.

"We stay close to the road," Jones whispers. "In the cover. April and Mei will be on the road."

The plan holds for a few minutes. Until I hear April's yell. "Mei, get behind me!"

I run toward the sound, ignoring Jones's voice. He's

probably telling me to stop, so we can coordinate. It would be the smart thing to do. But my legs are responding by instinct. Large, flat leaves slap against my thighs and shins. My jeans absorb the dampness of the leaves, adding weight to every step. The water drips down to my socks; my feet slip around inside my shoes.

I keep running.

Behind me, I can hear two men panting. Tiny and Jones, probably. No one's shooting at me yet.

The panting grows closer as my chest tightens. My legs feel rubbery.

"For fuck's sake," Jones whispers, next to me now. His hand closes around my arm, pulling me down.

Thirty yards away, I can see April in a clearing. She's a green shape in my goggles. Her back is to a tree. I can't see Mei anywhere. Ten figures surround April in a circle, just like in all those Kung Fu movies. Except I doubt they'll wait politely to attack one at a time.

Jones taps me on the shoulder, then Tiny. He points to himself, then to the right of where April is making her stand. He's going to take the right flank. He motions for Tiny to take the left flank, and for me to go straight in. He holds up two fingers, then taps his watch. Start shooting in two minutes. That I can do. Jones and Tiny are swallowed by the jungle as they move away. I creep closer, choosing each step carefully. The wet undergrowth hides the sounds of my approach.

I check my watch. Thirty seconds to go. April and her circle of attackers are only ten yards away. I know I'll only get one clean shot. On the second shot, they'll be able to triangulate me. Then I'll have to dodge and shoot.

One more step forward, then another. Something furry jumps out, hissing and squeaking. I manage to bite back my surprised yell, but it doesn't matter. The slight sound was enough to make the closest man turn. His bullet puts a hole in the leaf next to my foot. I fire back and hear a grunt, then duck behind a tree for cover. I don't know how badly he's hit.

The fireworks have started on either side of me. Through the goggles, I see two green shapes fall on my right, one shape on my left. All three are too large to be April. I hope she's taken cover. I risk a glance around the tree. A man's stumbling forward, holding one arm tight to his stomach. April's shape is nowhere in sight.

I spin out from behind the tree, crouching low, and fire. I see a spray of green from his forehead, the heat of blood. Two shots to kill one man. I can't afford that sort of math.

I hear yelling in Cantonese between Hu's men, hard to understand over the gunfire. I find a new hiding spot, behind a frond of palm leaves. The circle of men is smaller now, facing outward to defend themselves. April isn't among them. *Where is she?* Four bodies lie scattered on the jungle floor in the clearing. Five if you count the man at my feet. That should leave five more in the clearing . . . but there are only four. Never mind. Kill them. Find April.

I raise my gun, but stop short of firing. The fifth man has stepped into the clearing, holding someone in front of him. It's Hu, with a gun to April's head.

"Stop firing," Hu tells his men. "I have what they want."

We were so close.

"Come on out, Dan," Hu says. "And your CIA friend too. Drop your guns where I can see them."

He doesn't say anything about Tiny. Could it be he doesn't know? Or is Tiny dead?

Jones shows himself, holding only a pistol. Where's the automatic rifle? He follows Hu's orders, drops the pistol at the edge of the clearing. The glow stick is gone from the pocket of his vest. He's left the automatic rifle in the forest, marked with the glow stick. So Jones thinks Tiny is alive and can get to the second automatic rifle. Or he hopes. I can't leave my gun for Tiny. I only have the one.

"Take their goggles," Hu tells his men.

My goggles are torn off, taking some hair with them. Jones gets similar treatment. Without the goggles, I can see April's face clearly. She's not crying or struggling. The set of her jaw reminds me of when she was ten and faced down the neighborhood bully. William grounded her for not running to him for help, but you could secretly tell he was proud. April hasn't given up. She's waiting for the right time to make her move.

They take the knife sheathed at Jones's leg and throw it into the forest. It glitters under a bright moon. We're both searched, roughly, for other weapons.

"Where's Tiny?" Hu demands.

Jones smiles, almost serenely. "In a safe house. Telling one of my associates all your secrets."

"Trying to redeem yourself?" Hu asks Jones.

A muscle twitches in the agent's jaw. "Whatever you want to call it."

"You looked the other way for years because we could help each other. I want to start one little bank, and now we are enemies?"

"We were never friends," Jones says.

"Then maybe it will hurt less knowing you failed."

Jones laughs. Even Hu looks surprised.

"I didn't fail," Jones says. "With what Tiny is telling us, we can dismantle your business. None of your suppliers will ever work with you again."

Hu's gun twitches toward Jones before he remembers himself. "This is the part where you tell me I should let you go because someone knows where you are and killing an agent will make things worse for me."

Jones shrugs. "No. You know the drill. I die on assignment; they disavow all knowledge of me." He must have ice in his veins. I can feel a trail of sweat following the curve of my spine.

The kingpin's eyes narrow in frustration. "Never mind," Hu says. "I've seen your like before. I'm going to feed all three of you to the tigers. Even tough guys scream."

What the hell is Tiny waiting for?

"Her first, though." The fabric of April's shirt puckers as his hand tightens around her arm.

April winces; her pain stabs at my already broken heart.

"A child for a child," Hu says. "It is a fair trade."

A buzzing sound comes from Jones's vest. I jump, then curse myself for looking like an idiot. It's only his phone, vibrating in one of the pockets.

Hu smiles. "Someone is expecting to hear from you. The doting father, perhaps?"

"It is about that time," Jones says, louder than he needs to. He's signaling Tiny.

I look at April and find her green eyes unafraid. "Yes, it's time."

Tiny explodes from the underbrush, one automatic rifle in each hand, yelling some sort of declaration of love. April uses Hu's moment of distraction to drop clear of his arm, and roll backward between his legs. He aims his gun at us. Instead of rolling clear of him, April kicks both feet up, nailing him in the crotch. Jones and I dive for the ground just as Tiny starts shooting. I land in the muck face first. It smells like the gunk I pull out when the kitchen sink clogs. The gritty mud slips between my teeth, coats my tongue.

I spit it out and look up, careful to stay below the line of fire at chest level. I should help Tiny. Four men, including Hu, are still standing. They're all pulling up automatic rifles that match Tiny's. In the next second, he'll be outgunned. April crawls toward Hu, who has recovered from the blow to his groin. I wave her away; she shakes her head. There's no time to argue. If Tiny goes down, we all go down. I aim for the knees of goon one, knocking him to the side. I see Jones executing a similar maneuver out of the corner of my eye. Goon one pins me to the ground with a beefy arm and a knee on each thigh. He could be Tiny's little brother. He tries to bring up the automatic rifle to finish me off, but it's stuck underneath the paunch carefully cultivated by my lack of exercise. He gives up a split-second later; a knife appears in his hand. A heavy thud tells me Tiny got goon three.

The knife hovers over my neck, held back only by the

triangle of my arms. Goon one is stronger than I am. My muscles are shaking and his aren't. I wiggle one leg free and drive a knee into his ribs. He only grunts and pins me again. I try to roll but the suction of the mud holds me fast to the ground. My arms give a millimeter. The tip of the knife pricks my throat. I can't hold out much longer. His weight on my chest makes it hard to breathe.

This would be an honorable way to go. I saved April, didn't I? She has Tiny and Jones to get her out of here. She has everything ahead of her. What happens if I walk out of here? More nightmares. More drinking. More looking over my shoulder while I snitch on my clients to save my brother's hide. If I can even help my brother anymore. I doubt Hu kept it a secret I turned CIA informant.

I've been drinking myself to death for years anyway.

Goon one's skull cracks against Jones's knee. The knife falls, harmless, against my chest. The goon lands on his back next to me, dazed but not out. In one smooth motion, Jones picks up the knife on my chest and sends the point into the goon's throat. I feel the rush of wind, hear the whistle as it passes close to my arm. The mud near me becomes warm with my attacker's blood.

I sit up and the ground slurps, reluctant to let me go. Tiny is crouched on one knee, his hand pressed against something round and brown with mud. The back of Hu's head. His legs are kicking weakly. Tiny shows no signs of mercy. April hovers, like she might intervene.

"I should stop that," Jones says. "Protocol says I should bring Hu back for interrogation."

But Jones doesn't move. I think he wants to talk about it.

"Hu said you looked the other way."

"He dealt in blood diamonds," Jones says. "Useful when you need money that can be moved around in untraceable ways."

That's one side of Hu's business I never saw. Not that knowing about blood diamonds would have stopped me from taking his money. I'm disgusted by that person, as if it wasn't me a few days ago. Hu's fingers scrape at Tiny's hand in a last attempt to get free.

The fingers stop moving.

Jones shrugs.

April shivers.

I find enough strength to walk over to April, despite the headache starting at my temples. I turn her away from the dead body and Tiny's grim expression. She throws her arms around my neck, just like she did when she was little. I hope the shaking I feel is from adrenaline. After a long minute, she detaches herself.

"We have to get Mei," she says. "I told her to run."

Jones shakes his head. "There could be more of Hu's men out there."

"Exactly," April says.

"They're not after her."

"I will stay and look for her," Tiny declares. Except he looks a little bit tired. Drained. I wonder if killing his boss—well, ex-boss—did it. Or it could be the two circles of red spreading on his shoulder and his stomach. The mud was hiding his wounds. Jones and I step forward just in time to keep Tiny from falling to the ground. We both grunt when his weight falls on our arms; it feels like trying to catch a gorilla.

"He needs a hospital," Jones says. "Now."

April looks between the dense jungle and Tiny's pale face. "Mei! Mei!"

"Would you shut up? If anyone's out there, they'll know you're alive."

There's a rustling close to us, as if to prove Jones right. April looks scared. Jones drops his half of Tiny and picks up one of the fallen guns.

"It's only me," a nervous female voice says. "April? Are you there?"

"Mei!" April runs into Jones's outstretched arm.

"Let's make sure she's alone," Jones says.

Mei is alone. She looks scared, but cleaner than the rest of us.

"Now, can we try to be *quiet*," says Jones.

April nods.

Jones looks at the unfortunate Tiny. "One of us needs to be armed. Just in case. Can you two help Dan carry Ryan?"

We're not exactly graceful about it, but we make it to the road. Jones runs down to bring the car back. Tiny lies with his head in April's lap. His face doesn't show any pain.

"We made it," he says.

Her face is hard to read. "Yes. Almost. Just hang on."

Tiny tries, I can tell. But he passes out just as the car rounds the curve in the road. I feel for his pulse. Weak, but it's still there.

"He was willing to sacrifice himself for me," she says.

I don't know what to tell her. Sometimes that's enough for love, sometimes it's not. My third wife did everything she could to save me. I couldn't love her for it. Truth is, I only loved my first wife, Carol. The others I just tried hard.

Mei puts a hand on April's shoulder. "He seems nice, you know, for a gangster."

April smiles weakly. "Yeah, for a gangster."

CHAPTER 27

Dan
Hong Kong, 2015

I TAKE LOOKOUT duty, watching for any people or cars that might be coming up behind us. Tiny is propped up in the back seat with his tree trunk legs across my lap. I can't turn my body, just my head. After a few seconds, the odd angle makes my neck ache. But I don't look away.

The cars that carried Hu's men get smaller and smaller, then disappear around the curves in the road. No monsters jump out of the forest.

Mei and April are quiet in the front passenger seat. Jones is driving and, of course, on his phone again. This time, he's doing a lot more listening than talking.

"I understand, sir," he says.

We pass the marina with its bobbing lights. I still keep my head craned toward the back window. We were in such a rush, we didn't puncture the tires on the cars by the gate. If we didn't kill all of Hu's men, they could follow us. Even after we leave the back roads, with no one behind us, I can't look away. The night denizens of the city move around us on the streets. Flashy cars out for a night on the town. Second-shift workers slogging home on dark sidewalks.

"We don't need to do any cleanup, sir," Jones says.

The protests of my neck finally make me turn forward. In the rearview mirror, I see Jones roll his eyes, but his tone remains deferent.

"Only Ryan's fingerprints will be on the weapons." He's referring to Tiny. "We didn't touch the cars. By now, everyone connected will know Ryan turned against Hu. The confrontation at the zoo was just a failed exit interview. Ryan disappears, and everyone will think he ran." Jones looks annoyed at the reply. "If you wanted things to be done quietly, you should have given me more resources." Then he hangs up.

When we arrive at the hospital, a stretcher is waiting for Tiny with two agents to escort him. A cab is waiting too.

"Mei, that cab is for you," Jones says. "The driver is one of ours. You'll be taken to a safe house."

April watches Tiny get wheeled inside the hospital. I still can't read her feelings for him. After Tiny is swallowed by the glass doors, she gives Mei a hug.

April's wiping away tears as she gets back into the car.

"I never thanked you," she says to Jones.

The agent looks uncomfortable. "I got to settle an old score. Don't worry about it." He turns on the radio to fill the silence. The chatter of an overly enthusiastic spokesperson assaults my ears.

April's voice cracks as she tries to speak over the noise. "What should I do about Tiny?"

At this, Jones looks even more uncomfortable. "You want me to get him into the States with you? It's a little complicated. If you really want to be together—"

"No!" She shakes her head, then wrings her hands in her lap. "I mean, I don't want him hurt or anything but . . ."

"You want me to keep him away from you."

"Yes."

Well, that answers my questions about her feelings.

She looks at me, apologetic. "I know he was sort of your friend and all—"

Jones laughs. "Is that what Ryan told you?"

"Oh, good," she straightens. "He's not really my type."

"Thank God," I say.

"I'll take care of it," Jones says.

She looks suspicious. "Take care of it like you let Tiny take care of Hu?"

"Tempting, but no." Jones turns off the main road into a residential area. "We're going to the safe house where your parents are. You'll have a couple hours there, just until we get your flights arranged."

My gut twists. I don't want to see William and Marge. I found April, yes, but it's my fault she was in danger in the first place.

Jones pulls the car into a driveway in front of a small house. Lights shine out through the curtains. The fabric is pulled back, then falls into place again. The agent on guard, checking to see who's arrived. April gets out eagerly, then waits for me. When I don't leave the car, she opens my door. "You're coming in, right?"

"I'd rather not," I say.

"Don't be silly."

With an impatient sigh, Jones shuts the car off. "Do whatever you want, but I have to go inside for a while."

The last thing I want is to be alone with my thoughts. I follow Jones and April into the house. As soon as the door opens, William and Marge pull April into a hug. I study a generic picture of Buddha on the wall to look away from the little nuclear family. It's what I was trying for, all those years after Carol. Trying to recreate how Carol and I should have turned out but didn't.

It's a good thing we never had kids. God knows how a kid I raised would have turned out.

The happy family moves out of the entryway. My feet squish in my shoes. I slip them off, then see the mess we've made of the floor. The neat rubber mat is crowded with muddy shoes; the white linoleum is marked with dark brown footprints.

From the other room, I hear April say she's going to shower and change. The television is on too. I imagine them waiting the long hours, watching anything to pass the time.

Someone clears their throat next to me. I look up to see a stone-faced William. I recognize the expression from when we were kids. When he didn't know how to feel or how to handle a situation, he would hide behind that expression.

One commercial passes on the television. Then two. "I'm glad you made it," William says.

That's something. "I'm sorry we're late. I know you must have been worried."

He nods, glances behind him. "Marge says I should thank you. I'm not sure." There's the William I know.

"You're welcome."

"You've learned something, I hope."

I'm too tired, dehydrated, and hungry to finish this argument. I push past him. "I'm thirsty."

William blocks me. "April's safe. You're off liquor. Starting now."

I clench my teeth, remind myself he's trying to help in his own clumsy way. "I meant water." Because I did.

"Sure you did."

"Will," Marge says quietly, appearing behind him.

His mouth drops open. "After what he's done? After what nearly happened to our daughter?"

"Can't you see he's exhausted? Give him a little time to rest."

My brother throws his hands in the air. "Later, later. Always later. That's what you said for years. And then Mack is dead and my brother is running away—"

I thought I already explained this. "I didn't run away."

"Fine," he snaps. "You didn't run away. But you sure didn't try to help yourself either. You think it was easy after you left? Everyone thinks you were a dirty cop."

I let out a long breath. "Easier than me staying."

"April missed you," William says. "You just left. Not one word of goodbye."

"You missed him too," Marge says to William.

His mask of anger cracks. "Yeah, well."

"We all missed you," Marge says. "You're family."

I'm not quite sure what to say. Maybe this is why William prefers to argue. "I didn't really have a choice. I'm sorry." I'm glad April's still in the shower. When William and I argue, it always ends in yelling.

William shakes his head, back to being angry. "You were always sorry. You never could help yourself. April's safe. But from now on, you'll stay away from her until you've cleaned up your act."

Pink tinges Marge's cheeks. I don't see her angry often. "That's enough for now. You two can talk more later."

William storms on. "Why are you always defending him? Always telling me to forgive him? Give him a second chance, then a third—"

"You never gave me a second chance," I hear myself say. "You wrote me off after the birthday party, remember?"

His voice is so loud it echoes in the small entryway. "You know how much business I lost that day? Nobody wanted to hire the contractor whose brother wrecked their car."

I raise my voice to his volume and find my lips forming in a snarl that matches his. "You think it was easy being your brother?"

"Go ahead, blame me. It's always someone else's fault."

I thought my anger over Mack was gone. It's not. "You never missed a chance to tell me I should be more like Mack. What a piece of crap I was. You kept telling me how worthless I was until I believed it."

William looks shocked. "I was just trying . . ."

"You don't know what you do to people sometimes," Marge says gently. "Even when you mean well."

If I want William's forgiveness, I guess I should start with my own. Still, the words don't come out easily. "I know I was a piece of shit back then. I get now that you were trying to push me to get help."

William crosses his arms and steps back to study me. "I guess I didn't do it the right way."

"Well?" Marge says. She pushes William toward me. "You know what to do."

My brother holds out a hand. "Thank you for saving April. And I'm sorry. For everything."

Jones watches from across the room and rolls his eyes. Fuck him. I shake William's hand.

"I hate to interrupt the family special, but we have some business to conclude." He turns to the agent who made himself invisible during our argument. "Take them to the airstrip once April's ready. Dan and I are going to the hospital. Ryan's out of surgery."

CHAPTER 28

Dan
Hong Kong, 2015

JONES AND I walk through the organized chaos of the emergency room to the recovery wing. The hospital is familiar in an unnerving way. My parents died in a place like this. I visited friends who were shot on the job in a place like this. The air is sharp with antiseptic, a reminder of all the small things that can kill us. The long white hallway is only interrupted by the metallic gleam of a wheelchair, waiting for a patient. In most of the rooms, despite the late hour, I can hear televisions instead of conversations. Pain has a way of making you feel lonely and separate from the world. Doubly so in a place where every surface echoes the beep of machines, the scrape of paper, or the cough of someone down the hall.

An overworked nurse, head bent over his paperwork, guards a desk with a sign-in book for visitors. Jones raps on the counter to get his attention. "I need to speak to the doctor who operated on Ryan Sing."

The nurse, annoyed at the interruption, consults a computer screen. "I'll have her paged. You can wait over there." He points to a few hard plastic chairs lined up against the wall.

Jones paces. I sit. The doctor arrives five minutes later, holding a cup of coffee in one hand and a bag of seaweed chips in the other.

Her eyes note our muddy, disheveled appearance. "Can you make this quick?" she asks. "I've been on my feet for six hours, and my break is only ten minutes long."

"Is he lucid? Or are the pain meds still wearing off?"

"He can understand you and answer questions. Is that it?" She lifts her cup pointedly. "The vending machine coffee doesn't taste any better cold."

"Will he remember what we say?"

"Yes." She arches her eyebrows, curious.

Jones doesn't answer her implied question. "How badly was he injured?"

"The shoulder was a through and through. The shot in his midsection punctured the lower intestine. We stitched him back up."

Jones frowns, though I doubt his concern is for the patient's welfare. "Can he be transported?"

"The sooner you get him out of here, the better." She leaves the rest unsaid. I'm familiar with her expression. I saw it every time we took a suspect to the hospital when I was on the force. The doctors were bound by their oaths; they saved murderers and arsonists and abusers stabbed by their victims in self-defense. But they didn't have to like it. It's almost enough to make me feel sorry for Tiny.

"Thanks," Jones says. "We'll get him moved."

"He's in the room around the corner. Just look for the badges," she says, already walking away.

We turn the corner and see the agents guarding Tiny's room. They nod to Jones and let us pass. There's another bed in the room, but it's empty.

Tiny's sipping water, eyeing the guards at the door suspiciously. He smiles when he sees us. I don't return the expression. I don't know how to feel about Tiny. Sure, he saved April. But that was after he kidnapped her.

"April is okay?" he asks.

I take one of the chairs by the bed, the same hard plastic ones that were in the hallway. "Yeah, the family's on their way home."

"You'll be taken to a safe house to finish your recovery," Jones tells Tiny. "Then in a few days, we'll relocate you."

Tiny picks at the wrinkles in the white sheets. "Did April give you a message for me? Can I call her from the safe house?"

I lean back, interested to see what magic trick Jones has up his sleeve.

Jones perches on the edge of the bed. "April hasn't figured out how she feels about you. And it might be better to leave it at that."

"But I love her!"

Jones starts to roll his eyes, then summons his patience. "Think about it, Ryan."

"I asked you to call me Clint."

"Clint." Jones takes another breath. "You were Hu's right-hand man for nearly twenty years. You're marked now. It's not just Hu's secrets you know, but the secrets of half of the people he worked with. You'll be looking over your shoulder for the rest of your life."

Tiny drops his head to his chest. "It would be dangerous for her."

"Better to let her move on. Before she gets more involved."

"But I . . ." Tiny's eyes mist over.

Okay, I officially feel sorry for him. I wonder if Jones has a backup plan. Jones taps a finger against his leg, outside of Tiny's view. The sympathetic expression on Jones's face doesn't betray his impatience.

Tiny sets his shoulders and swallows hard. "You're right, I must stay away from her because I love her. To protect her."

I try not to look relieved.

"It's like in the great Westerns," Tiny continues. "I must ride off into the sunset."

Jones coughs; I think he's trying not to laugh. "Yeah, just like that."

We say our goodbyes quickly. There's no point in either of us pretending we'll see Tiny again. Jones still hasn't told me what his plans for me are. I'm afraid to ask. So I don't say anything when Jones steers the car onto the highway. Wherever we're going, it's away from the city. The lights get farther apart. The buildings get shorter and space themselves out. He turns down a series of twisting, unmarked roads. Our ride ends at a long strip of concrete with a plane waiting. A small, private plane like the one executives might charter.

I guess I knew I had to leave. I never really liked Hong Kong anyway. But I figured out how to survive here. Mostly.

Jones leaves the keys in the car when he gets out. He

takes a few steps, then turns around, a silhouette against the landing lights of the plane. "Well?"

It's not like I have anything else to do.

I stumble on the last step into the plane, surprised to see April, William, and Marge. Marge and April are sleeping soundly. William acknowledges me with a nod. The luxury days of this plane have clearly passed. The upholstery is scratched. The plastic has yellowed.

The pilot appears from the cockpit. "Everyone here?" the pilot asks. He has the same surly demeanor as Jones.

"Yeah," Jones says. "Let's get the fuck out of here." He digs around in a tiny closet and pulls out two towels and a collection of clothes. "I'm showering first. Then you. You stink."

The pilot looks back. "You're not supposed to be in the bathroom during takeoff and landing."

Jones salutes him with one finger as he closes the bathroom door.

"Whatever." The pilot sighs. He stops again, just before shutting the cockpit door. "If you fall and crack your head open, I'm not helping until we reach cruising altitude." There's no response from Jones. I wonder how Marge and April are sleeping, until I see the white plugs in their ears.

William holds up his own pair. "Specially made for airplanes. Pilot swears by them. Says I'll rest like a baby." He puts them in his ears, then closes his eyes. I don't know if he's feigning sleep or not. I decide I don't care. Silence is easier than talking.

Jones is out of the shower before we reach cruising altitude. I follow the pilot's directions and wait. I have to swallow to make my ears pop. William, Marge, and April stir, but don't wake. Even relaxed, the bags under their eyes show the stress of the day. Once we level out, I squeeze myself into the doll-sized bathroom. I have to perch the clean clothes on top of the toilet, next to the basket of toiletries packaged like fast food condiments.

The showerhead is doll-sized too, but at least the water is hot. I use two packets of shampoo and three of bodywash. I brush my teeth under the water until my gums hurt, but I can still taste the mud. I can still see Hu's legs kicking.

Jones pounces on me the second I step out of the bathroom. "Interview time."

"Can I eat first?" I ask pointedly. Jones might be a machine, but I'm not.

"You can eat while we talk." He points to a tray he's set by my seat. There are various plastic packages of food that don't expire: crackers, jerky, dried fruit. There are also two bottles of water, just for me.

I consider ignoring him, but only for a second. A bulldog is less stubborn.

"It'll only be a couple hours," he says. It's almost an apology. "I'm off to another assignment when we land. My team went through your files. I just need to fill in some holes."

I answer his questions between bites and gulps. The food runs out, and I finish both bottles of water. An hour later, my throat is so dry I'm coughing every other sentence. Jones glances at William, reclined in his seat. "I think there's a beer in the fridge," he says.

William snores softly, as if to answer my question. I lumber over to the small fridge. There's one beer, in the back.

And it's a good one, not like my roommate's swill. It keeps me going a little bit longer, but soon I can barely finish a sentence without yawning.

Jones rubs a hand over his face; he's fading too. "All right. I think we're done here. Sign your statement."

I sign it without reviewing what Jones wrote. It's not that I trust him; I just can't summon the energy to care. There's another unpleasant matter to be settled. I hand the stack of pages back to Jones. "It was nice of you to put me on the same plane as my brother, but I don't think I should go back to Philadelphia. You'll have to drop me off somewhere else."

William stirs; I hide the empty beer can by my feet. Did he hear Jones offer it to me?

"Your personal problems aren't my concern," Jones says. "Philadelphia's a big city. You're a big boy. You can leave and go elsewhere."

"It's not that."

"You're not a danger to April or the family. You're not in the same position Tiny is." He snaps the paperwork into a folder, then into a leather briefcase. If I hadn't seen him kill four people today, I could mistake him for a tired secretary after a long shift. "You're small fry in comparison. I doubt Hu's successor will think twice about you unless you're stupid enough to visit Hong Kong."

I hadn't considered whether being geographically close to April and her family would pose a threat to them. It seemed a moot point, considering I'll spend the rest of my life in federal prison if I step inside the United States again. "Better to be safe," I say.

Jones sighs. "Is this about the paperwork you filed to renounce your US citizenship?"

"Sort of."

"I think we can count that as your only unsuccessful divorce."

"What?" I remember signing the damning forms. The governor-then-senator's lawyers brought them to me in the holding cell to make sure I could imagine where I'd be living if I refused.

He's writing a note in large letters on a blank piece of paper. "You sent in the oath of renunciation via mail. That's not valid. You have to appear in person at an embassy."

Technically, I didn't send it in. The lawyers did. The bastards never told me it didn't count. Not that it changes much. "Still, I can't go back. Not anywhere in the United States."

Jones's hand pauses on the lever to recline his chair. "Fine. Whatever. We're stopping to refuel in L.A. When we land in Philadelphia, we'll talk. I need some sleep." He lies back, attaches the note to a thin blanket with a paperclip, then pulls the blanket over himself.

The note is addressed to Steven. Must be the pilot.

No, I will not return my seat to the upright position for landing, asshole.

I wish I could get away with the same thing.

CHAPTER 29

Dan
Philadelphia, 2015

IT'S THE SCENT of the air that wakes me when we land. Less soy sauce. Less fish. Less smog. More french fries. I'm in the United States.

I open my eyes. Marge and April are gone. I won't get a chance to say goodbye. William is neatly folding the blanket he used. He never folds anything. He's been waiting for me to wake up.

"Welcome home," my brother says.

It's a nice sentiment. "I can't stay."

I hear a rustle and look to my left, expecting to see Jones still asleep. Instead he's on the phone again. He doesn't look like he's rested at all. Not that I look like a winner, I'm sure.

"You're getting off here," Jones says.

"But I told you—"

Jones glares at William. "Your brother kept me awake

explaining your situation. Asked if I could clear things up for you."

That's not at all like the William I know.

"He's a persistent son of a bitch," Jones says.

William smiles his best CEO smile, the one he uses when difficult contract negotiations have come out in his favor.

"But the senator's connections—"

"Senator Holden died of a heart attack in bed with an underage prostitute three years ago. Even you couldn't damage his reputation now."

Hope flares up before I remember myself. I had reasons to stay away. It can't possibly be this simple. "Mack was tied in with the mob. They hold a grudge."

"Against a dirty cop?"

I'm ready to slug him. "I never helped them."

Jones eyes me warily. "I've been on the phone for the past three hours. Everyone at Philadelphia PD and the DA's office thinks you and Mack were working together and that you ran to avoid prosecution. They think all the evidence against you was destroyed because of your 'connections.' I'm sure Senator Holden's people arranged it that way."

I suppose the department thinking I'm a coward is better than the mob thinking I'm a threat.

"The DA can't make a case against you because all the evidence was destroyed. I wouldn't expect to get out of any speeding tickets, but you'll be fine as long as you keep your head down."

"You mean as long as I let my former coworkers think I'm as dirty as my partner was."

"You have a place to stay in Philadelphia," Jones says. "That's more than you have anywhere else."

A place to stay? I look at William. "You'll have me in your home?"

"You'll get sober," William says.

"You'll be patient."

"No promises," my brother and I say at the same time.

Jones claps us both on the back forcefully. I think he's pushing us toward the door. "Look at that. Two assholes in a pod."

I feel like I should have something to carry off the plane. I don't. Everything from my former, temporary life is back in my apartment in Hong Kong.

"Thanks," I tell Jones.

This time Jones actually pushes us toward the door. "Now would you get off the plane so I can get some sleep?"

William and I step into the early evening onto yet another runway. The plane's engine revs up. The dark is jarring. Like it's been dark for an entire day. But that's just what happens when you come back from the other side of the world.

I follow William to the small parking lot next to a shed. Marge is loading luggage into a cab. Courtesy of Jones, I'm sure.

For an asshole, he's not so bad. I catch myself smiling slightly in the rearview mirror as the cab pulls away. It's hard to imagine why. I just had my last beer four hours ago. I have no savings and the best job I'll get here is minimum wage. I don't have any references I can use. I'll be living at my brother's house; the only thing we're good at is fighting.

Knowing my luck, I'll run into Carol at the grocery store and she'll see just how right she was to divorce me.

Still, it's home.

THE CHAPTER BLANK PAGE

Knowing my luck, I'll run into Carol at the grocery store
and she'll ask how, right, he was to divorce me.
Still. It's home.

CHAPTER 30

Kevin
Washington, DC, 2023

KEVIN PATTED DENTON on the cheek. "Time to wake up."

Denton groaned as he opened his eyes. "What the—" He struggled against the ropes that tied his wrists and ankles to the chair.

"You're safe as long as you don't yell," Kevin said.

"Release me right now," Denton said through gritted teeth. "Or I will have you arrested for treason after I end your career." He did a double take as he noticed the man, not tied to his chair, sitting next to him. "Who the hell are you?"

Kevin leaned next to the carefully folded dry cleaning bag. The closet in this fancy hotel room was bigger than the bathroom in his apartment. "In a few minutes, your informant is going to knock on the door of this hotel room. I know you think he's a police officer in Hong Kong. But he's really Hu's son."

"Hu. The guy who ran the Little Caesar gang?" Denton looked past the open closet doors to the gilded curtains and the ornately curved furniture. He jerked at his ropes again and then studied the stranger calmly sitting next to him.

Kevin could see Denton's thoughts, clear as day: how strongly was the stranger Kevin's ally? Could Denton convince the stranger to help him instead?

"Yes, the gang you thought was run by Ryan Sing, aka Tiny Clint," Kevin said.

"Okay, fine, you were right about that," Denton said. "Hu ran the gang. I found the real police reports. But my informant can't be Hu's son. Hu's son died, you said so yourself."

Kevin checked his watch. Timing was everything on this little play he'd put together. "I thought so too. That was my mistake. I figured no one could survive that sort of injury." Kevin remembered what Hu had said while threatening April. *A child for a child. It is a fair trade.* Hu had told Kevin his son had died.

"Your story does seem implausible." The stranger spoke for the first time.

"I appreciate you giving me the chance to prove my case," Kevin said. "Denton Carlisle, I'd like you to meet a representative of the General Office. He's requested I not share his name. But for your benefit, the General Office is—"

"An arm of the Chinese Communist Party." Denton glared at Kevin. "I'm not an idiot."

Kevin turned off the closet lights. "As I said, in a few

minutes Hu's son is going to arrive. He and I are going to have a conversation."

Denton's chair shifted as he tested Kevin's knots again. "This little stunt won't go unreported."

"If you'd like to join that conversation, feel free to make some noise and let him know you're here," Kevin continued. "But this is likely the same man that killed and dismembered Tiny Clint. So if I were you, I'd keep your mouth shut."

"You piece of—" Denton cut himself off and took two deep, deliberate breaths.

Kevin glanced at the defibrillator he'd stocked in the corner. Just in case Denton's legendary poise fractured into a heart attack.

"Let's say you're right," Denton said. "You think you're going to have a short, pleasant conversation with Hu's son. And then he's just going to what? Walk away?"

"That's exactly what's going to happen," Kevin said.

"You're fucking insane," Denton said.

Kevin smiled. "No, I'm just good at my job." He heard the knock on the door. Carefully, he shut the closet doors just enough for Denton and the CCP representative to have a crack to see through. "Enjoy the show."

If things didn't work out Kevin's way, Kevin wouldn't be alive to see Denton gloating. It was a small comfort.

Kevin opened the door to see Hu Gao, the son of the man Kevin had watched suffocate to death in the mud. Gao was trim with dark hair styled with the carefully tousled appearance of a K-pop star. His outfit was all designer rip-off pieces. A man with aspirations, who felt like the world had cheated him out of his legacy. In other words, a very dangerous man.

"Kevin Fellows."

"Please, come in," Kevin said.

As Gao brushed past him, Kevin studied the suit jacket and wide-legged pants further. Where would Gao hide the knife rumors said he carried everywhere?

"How did you find me?" Gao asked.

"I followed Denton to a meeting with you," Kevin said. "I was very surprised. No one thought you were alive."

"So you know who I am."

Would Gao cling to the story he gave Denton? "I have a guess," Kevin said.

"Tell me, then," Gao said. "Who am I and how do I know you?"

"You've been living under another name and working at the Ministry of Public Security for the CCP. But your real name is Hu Gao, son of the legendary patriarch of the Little Caesar Gang. I used to work with your father."

"You addressed me correctly," Gao said. "Family name first, then surname."

Gao hadn't contradicted Kevin. Would that be enough proof for Denton? No, Denton would want an explanation for why Gao was still alive.

"I was hoping we could have a respectful conversation," Kevin said. "You have your father's strength. You must be a man of extraordinary will to survive what you survived."

"My father was a smart man, always thinking ahead," Gao said.

Kevin waited. Gao clearly wanted an audience; Kevin would play along.

"We screened our security services for blood type. And when the time came, like all great leaders, my father demanded their sacrifice."

"Your father sacrificed one his employees to replace the blood you lost." Kevin shouldn't be surprised. Hu had been vicious and cunning and self-centered. In Hu's mind, the world owed him everything.

"He sacrificed himself willingly."

Kevin doubted that was true. But he wouldn't contradict Gao. The old lessons from Hong Kong were returning. So strongly Kevin had to mentally steady himself. All those meetings in Hu's warehouses arranging for CIA goods to move along with Hu's shipments. Moving untraceable money with blood diamonds. Hu valued deference in his allies. Kevin would let Gao think he was in charge too. Until Kevin had what he wanted.

"But you're right," Gao continued. "It was my strength that pulled me through in the end. The surgeons didn't think they could save me, even though they knew my father said he would kill them for failing."

That explains why Hu thought his son was dead. Hopefully that was enough for Denton to believe Kevin. Now for his second task: convince the CCP that Gao was a liability. The CCP wouldn't want one of their own resurrecting the Little Caesar gang.

"You wanted leverage over me," Kevin said. "Now you have it. What do you want?"

"Have you considered maybe I just want revenge?" Gao asked. "You killed my father."

"I tried to save him." That was a lie, but only two living people knew it. The other person was Dan Mackenzie; Kevin trusted him to keep the secret. Kevin deliberately cast his eyes down just far enough to show deference, but not far enough to miss Gao reaching for a weapon. "You know how strong Tiny Clint was. I couldn't pull him away."

Gao circled Kevin. "I don't believe you. Even if I did, you worked against my father. My father's arrangement with the CIA was profitable. And you ended it."

Kevin wondered how much Gao knew. Clearly, Gao knew Kevin had been involved. What files had Gao seen? What information had Denton let slip in meetings with Gao? Best to go with details no official report contradicted. "Under orders, unfortunately," Kevin said. This was mostly true. Kevin's anonymous tip had led to the reporter asking around which led to the decision that dealing with Hu would be too risky. But Gao couldn't possibly have traced that.

"You are good at following orders," Gao said.

The irony nearly made Kevin smile. Clearly, Gao had never seen any of Kevin's performance reviews. "I didn't enjoy being set against your father," Kevin said. "But when the agency heard about the bank the Little Caesar gang wanted to start, I was pulled in."

Gao rested one hand in his pocket. Kevin calculated the distance between them. How much time would he have to react if Gao pulled out his knife?

Offer him what he wants, Kevin thought. "Your father

built an empire; I respected him for it." Kevin had respected Hu, in a way. Power had been a weapon in Hu's hands. Kevin had watched as Hu moved men like marionettes to build a criminal empire. But Hu had had strings Kevin pulled on too. Flattery had always worked to earn his trust. "It must have been hard to get rid of all the evidence Hu was in charge and make it look like Ryan Sing was," Kevin said. "You certainly convinced Denton."

"Not so hard," Gao said. "I was inspired by your January 6. In the Ministry of Public Security, we've spent years trying to erase the memory of Tiananmen Square. But within weeks, your politicians were rewriting history."

Everyone in the intelligence community had been rattled by January 6. The agency was used to observing, sometimes orchestrating, violent coups in other nations. Not so close to home. Not so close they would possibly end up working for the overthrower. "They were." Kevin said. "Because he still controlled the party. And they wanted to keep their jobs."

"Exactly," Gao said. "Power speaks to power. The CCP was more than happy to see my father's legacy erased; it removed a liability for them."

Of course. Kevin hadn't seen that angle. He should be careful not to underestimate Gao.

"I saved all the records I told them I destroyed," Gao said. "I can rewrite history again later."

Gao wanted the same power his father had had. Kevin needed Gao to say all that out loud though. Or the CCP wouldn't rein Gao in.

"Your father owned half of Hong Kong," Kevin said.

"He could make anyone do anything." A slight exaggeration, but Kevin knew Gao would appreciate it.

"We took over most of the gangs in the city. Their leaders worked against us, then we took them out and their lieutenants worked for us," Gao said. "He used to say the best revenge is servitude."

So close. Kevin needed Gao's grandiose ambitions to be explicit. "You have plans for me."

"I make this internal investigation against you go away," Gao said. "But in return, you work for me. So when I rebuild my father's empire, you and I can make sure the CIA doesn't get in the way."

"What about the Chinese Communist Party?" Kevin asked. "I don't think they'll want to be associated with a new criminal enterprise in Hong Kong. Especially not when they're trying to keep the international community from interfering in their governance changes."

"By the time they know anything, I will be powerful enough to deal with them," Gao said.

Gao had said everything Kevin needed him to say. Kevin wanted to take a bow, but he kept his slightly dejected expression. Time to dismiss Gao before the situation went sideways.

"Make this OIG case go away, and I am at your service," Kevin said.

"I won't forget how you failed my father," Gao said. "Do not fail me."

Gao had no idea his future was already over. But Kevin would keep playing the part until Gao left. Kevin nodded, still slumped and seated on the bed.

The second the door shut behind Gao, Kevin straightened. He walked to the door and engaged the deadbolt. Just in case.

Kevin's cell phone vibrated; Saul's text message reporting Gao was in the lobby.

"It's safe to leave the closet now," Kevin said.

The CCP representative pushed open the closet doors. "We appreciate you bringing this problem to our attention. As you know, the CCP doesn't tolerate crime in our midst."

Unless it benefits the party, Kevin thought. "I'm always happy to cooperate when our mutual interests align."

The CCP representative nodded curtly then left. Kevin was alone with the guy he'd drugged and tied to a chair. A guy Kevin now needed to be on his side.

This day wasn't done with Kevin yet.

Kevin pulled out his knife and approached Denton slowly. "I'm going to cut you free now."

Denton's glare deepened into a snarl. "You fucking better."

Kevin left the knife on the floor with the bits of rope that fell there. Denton would feel safer that way. With his arms held up slightly and his palms open, Kevin backed away. "You're free to go."

Denton made it halfway to the door before he turned around, just as Kevin knew he would.

"This doesn't change anything." A fleck of spit followed Denton's words. "You don't even know why you're actually in trouble for that operation, do you?"

"I think I do." Cold. Ruthless. Effective. Difficult. All words that had been used to describe Kevin at one time or another. He knew he didn't see the world the way other people saw it. "I was supposed to bring Hu in for questioning. He died in the operation. We lost intel."

"You didn't follow orders," Denton said. "Hu was your target. You prioritized saving April, Dan, even Ryan Sing over bringing Hu in."

Kevin smiled. "That's what you think happened. But you can't prove it. Your informant wasn't who he said he was. You have no reliable witnesses."

"*I'm* a reliable witness," Denton said. "You kidnapped me. Are you going to call me a liar when I write that up?"

"You won't," Kevin said. "You're welcome, by the way."

Two long strides brought Denton in front of Kevin.

He moves fast when he wants to. And now Denton was exactly where Kevin wanted him. Farther from the door, further into this conversation. Where Kevin was in control.

"What could I possibly thank you for?" Denton asked.

"For saving your reputation," Kevin said. "You were building a case with false statements from a compromised source. At the very least, it would have come out that your source worked in the Ministry of Public Security. You would have looked foolish. Or worse, like a stooge for the CCP."

"So you kidnapped me."

"You wouldn't have believed me," Kevin said. "You can report me if you like, but then you'll have to explain how I discovered your informant was lying instead of you."

Frustration reddened Denton's cheeks.

Kevin didn't need an answer; he knew Denton wouldn't report him. Denton could be useful too, in his own way. Denton was predictable, most people were. After enough operations, Kevin had learned to see people according to their motivations and their capabilities. And he knew how to assemble people into a mechanism to apply leverage to achieve an objective.

"It's okay, you don't have to like me. Or thank me." Kevin stood. "No one thanked me for the Hong Kong operation either."

Denton had recovered his composure. "You brought back the wrong target. We needed intel from Hu, not his lieutenant."

"Hu knew how to play us," Kevin said. "If he'd survived, he would have given up just enough information for us to let him go and then he would have continued selling his services to the highest bidder. Ryan Sing knew most of what Hu knew, but all Ryan wanted to do was disappear. He was more honest with us and wasn't going to work against us after we let him go."

"So you did let Hu die," Denton said. "You ignored your orders."

"I'm merely suggesting that the target I did bring back was more useful for us," Kevin said. "All you have is speculation."

"Fuck. Off." Denton slammed the door on the way out. His anger was actually a good sign. It meant Denton knew Kevin was right. About reporting the "kidnapping." About the threat Gao posed to Denton's reputation.

Kevin stretched his arms and sat down on the bed. He gave himself a minute to lie back on the ridiculously expensive mattress. Checkout time was 11:00 a.m. the next morning. He could spend the evening here and take a long bath in the soaker tub with gold-plated fixtures. He could have the chef paged to create any Hong Kong delicacy he could think of. Tempting. But Kevin was nothing if not disciplined.

Staying around was a risk. With no practical reward.

A message interrupted his thoughts. Kevin gritted his teeth. Saul probably, needing some reassurance. But when he checked his phone he found a message from Navy instead.

> *Saul said it's a wrap. You good? Jackson and Irving are worried to. He's doing laundry over here taking a break from the dorm. If you wanted to come over for dinner.*

Kevin reread the message. Dinner at Jackson and Navy's apartment with Irving. Kevin had been worried about leaving Irving alone. Irving was a freshman in college now, no longer a kid. But Kevin still had things to teach him. Jackson and Navy's apartment would be cramped with all four of them. Definitely less fancy. Still risky. Connections always were.

But that risk seemed worth the reward.

ACKNOWLEDGMENTS

Many years ago, I asked my cousin to sum up his impressions of Hong Kong in one sentence. His answer gave me the first line of the first chapter. Sometimes that's all it takes to start a book in my head. One line that led me to a bar in Hong Kong with a cop at the bottom of his luck and an intellectual enforcer with a heart of gold.

As I write this, I'm sitting in one of the most beautiful places in the world – in the woods by a lake in Northern Minnesota. I come up here for the scenery and for the quiet community. Like most places in the United States, there's history here. Indigenous people lived and hunted in the BWCA for centuries before European settlers and trappers arrived. Their overtrapping and habitat destruction tested the resilience of this ecosystem. With conservation efforts now in place, the BWCA is a wild place again. But not, I imagine, as wild as it once was. Destruction is always faster than recovery.

By and large, the people who now live and visit here want to keep the area beautiful and healthy. That's a conscious choice we all make every time we step into the woods or paddle onto the lake. We can make choices that build communities within ecosystems.

In "The Monk and the Robot" series by Becky Chambers, she imagines a world where humans have everything they need and most of the things they want. They don't live on the edge of ecological collapse. They consume thoughtfully and equitably instead of mindlessly. And, in return, they all have nice things. They make choices that protect people and the environment.

The people that have helped me along the way are those sorts of people. Each, in their own quiet way, is doing their best to repair the world a little. And I'm grateful they've given me a little bit of their attention. I dropped the ball and didn't get copies out to any of them early. But they still deserve to have their names listed here: Chris Gales, Bridget Kromhout, Ry4an Brase, and Kelly Stahlberg.

My editor, Heidi Peterson, took on this complicated manuscript with grace. She pushed me to sharpen my words, even in the parts I thought had polished already. All remaining mistakes are mine.

I owe thanks to everyone mentioned here for supporting the imaginary communities in my head.